Love's Master

NEW YORK TIMES BESTSELLING AUTHOR

K.M. SCOTT

WRITING AS GABRIELLE BISSET

Published in the United States
ISBN-10: 1941594182
ISBN-13: 978-1-941594-18-6

Cover design: Cover Me, Darling

Interior designed and formatted by

E.M.
TIPPETTS
BOOK DESIGNS

www.emtippettsbookdesigns.com

Adult Content: Contains adult sexual content

Love's Master

Twenty-three year old Lily finds herself widowed and forced to live with her brother and his family, including his eight year old son William, who is nothing short of a terror. Sure she cannot go another day with his behavior, she begins to search for a new nanny and tutor for her nephew with little success. But when she happens across an advertisement in the Times that seems to be the answer to her problem, she is set on a path that will take her where she's never been before. Victorian England is a place of strict social codes, and the sensual world she enters is strictly forbidden for a woman of her social stature.

Her guide in this world is a man named Kadar, and the feelings he stirs in Lily threaten to change her forever. However, Victorian society is never far away, and her brother intends on seeing his sister remarried and settled into a home near him in Regent's Park. Lily will have to choose between Kadar, who makes her feel more alive than she ever believed she could, and Captain Mason Danvers, the gentleman who can offer her security and comfort for the rest of her life.

Love's Master

London, 1853

L ily sat in the parlor attempting to read a book and tried to tune out the din caused by her eight-year-old nephew. Repeatedly, he raced back and forth from the kitchen to where she sat, yelling and chasing the cat his parents had given him for his birthday one month earlier. In his wake were toys strewn all about that he'd discarded in favor of whatever else had attracted his attention. At the moment, it was the cat, which luckily could run faster on four legs than William could run on two.

While she loved her brother's child, she silently lamented the events of her life that had caused her to move in with him and his parents.

If only...

But recriminations wouldn't bring her husband back. Taken from her just three years into their marriage and before they could be blessed with a child of their own,

1

he'd been a victim of the cholera epidemic that had ravaged the city. Now a widow, she had few choices but to look to her family for support and a place to call home.

Her brother Richard and his wife Elizabeth had welcomed her with open arms, a fact she now suspected had hidden their happiness at the prospect of having an additional adult to tend to their son. The reality was that no one had ever truly tended to William, and as a result, the child was incorrigible. Nannies came and went with alarming speed, as did tutors who simply refused to deal with the child whose temper tantrums were legendary on Frederick Street. Few of their neighbors in the London suburb of Regent's Park had escaped the scene of the young boy's misbehavior.

"William!" she snapped as she caught him by the arm.

Stunned into stopping for a moment, he stood in front of his aunt and stared up into her eyes in surprise. Lily looked at the deceptively angelic face looking back at her, knowing the façade was just that. Beneath his rosy-cheeked expression was the terror of her new home.

Holding him, she said, "William, I want you to sit down this minute. I will not tolerate this behavior any more."

Smiling, the child replied sweetly, "All right, Aunty Lily," and when she released her hold on him, he promptly ran away screaming after the cat.

Two hours later, Lily was sure she couldn't stand another day of her nephew's behavior but was just as sure she'd have to be the one to tackle the issue if it were ever to be solved. Scouring the newspaper advertisements for

willing participants to replace the nanny and tutor, both of whom had recently left as their predecessors had, she recognized the names of many of the men and women who sought employment and knew no amount of money could entice them to return.

Sadly, she was forced to admit the solution to her problem wouldn't be found in the employment section of the Times. She continued to peruse the paper, at least hoping to find some diversion from the noise around her.

William walked up to her and tapped his hand on the newspaper. "Aunty Lily, play with me!"

Looking down at him, she wondered if a little guidance from her might do the trick. "If I do, you must promise to behave. Do you understand?"

"Yes, I promise."

With a great deal of direction, she found some measure of success in making him behave. When his parents finally returned from their time away nearly an hour later, she was set on broaching the discussion of what would have to be done with her nephew. If she didn't, she was convinced she'd soon go mad.

After a dinner that included more of William's bad behavior and a temper tantrum over the suggestion he eat his vegetables, his mother took him to prepare for bed and Lily took the opportunity to discuss the situation with her brother.

"Richard, I think something must be done with William."

Her brother looked past her, his face a practiced expression of feigned interest. "Everything will be better when we hire a new nanny and tutor."

"Please excuse my interference, but nothing is going to be better if William doesn't learn to behave."

The silence that met her statement along with the continued stare past her told Lily he knew she was right. It also told her that her suspicion was correct—if anything were to change, she would have to change it.

Touching his hand, she continued in a far softer tone. "Richard, I appreciate how much you've done for me since Jeremy's death. Let me help you with this."

Her brother sighed and seemed to admit defeat. "Fine. You may be in charge of finding a new nanny and tutor for William."

Lily rose to leave the table, but Richard stopped her. "I want to discuss something with you. I have someone I want you to meet. A gentleman."

"Why?"

"Lily, your mourning period has been over for months. You need to rejoin the world."

"I'm not out of the world, Richard."

"I invited Captain Mason Danvers to join us for dinner soon. He's a wonderful man, a veteran of the Army. I'm sure you'll like him."

Quietly, she said, "I'm not sure I'm ready."

"I understand how difficult this is for you, but you're a young woman who shouldn't be stuck living with her relatives."

Lily knew what her brother really meant was that as much as he loved her, he didn't want to be forced to baby-sit a grown woman for any longer than society dictated.

And that meant he was actively searching for a potential husband for her.

All she hoped was that his choice was someone she could grow to like.

For hours, she thought about the surprise life had thrown her. Married at nineteen to a man who had swept her off her feet, she had taken to the role of wife easily, believing the rest of her life had been plotted out for her as it was for other women lucky enough to be successfully married.

Jeremy had been the perfect husband, kind but with the ability to handle her stubborn streak. And as a lover, he'd been patient and devoted—just what any young woman would want to initiate her into the world of marriage.

She watched as the day faded into darkness remembering the feeling of having someone close as the night settled in. Sadness came over her as it always did when she thought about her husband's passing before they'd had the chance to have a child. Reconciled to a life without Jeremy, she'd turned to Richard for help.

But could she deal with the type of help he now offered? She sympathized with his desire to have her settled with another husband. Who wanted a twenty-three-year-old sister hanging about, especially a willful one? She couldn't change who she was, but would this Mason Danvers want her as much as Richard wanted him to?

Lily remembered meeting Captain Danvers once before when Richard and Elizabeth had insisted she attend the Jarret's Christmas party. Still in mourning, she'd relented and joined them, but looking back now, she was sure she hadn't made much of an impression dressed in her mourning clothes and wearing a look of sadness she'd accepted as fitting for a widow, even a young one.

He'd struck her as confident, if not a little too brash, and a man who probably wouldn't look twice at a woman like her, dressed in mourning garb or not. Tall and suntanned, with hair the color of caramel, he looked like a man who'd seen the world outside of England — the quintessential military man of the Empire. Lily, on the other hand, had always seen herself as the picture of English womanhood, with porcelain skin and brown hair. The only thing that set her apart from every other pale skinned brunette in London was the color of her eyes. Deep green, they told of an exotic ancestry long buried in the Scott family.

She'd never thought of herself as a beauty, no matter what Jeremy had said, and as the memory of Mason Danvers grew in her mind, she wondered if Richard's efforts to entice the man to marry her were all for naught. For what men like him preferred were women to compliment them. And she was not that woman in any sense of the word.

Lily sat with the newspaper in her lap, praying that someone new could be found among the advertisers she'd already been forced to dismiss as possibilities. A

fitful night's sleep tossing and turning while her mind raced over having to meet Captain Danvers caused her nerves to be on edge, and she was embarrassed to admit she dreaded William's impending arrival in the breakfast room. Desperate to find a new nanny or tutor, she buried her nose in the paper and began what she hoped would be a fruitful search.

The advertisements offered nothing, and as she sat dejected, she turned to the Agony Column, knowing at least she'd find kindred spirits in the lost lovers and desperate souls searching for that which life and circumstance had taken or failed to provide.

Even a brief perusal of the notices in this part of the Times provided a reader a glimpse into the often lonely world of the strangers who inhabited London and its suburbs. With any luck, Lily hoped to get lost in the world of these strangers so as to forget the one she'd been thrust into and which seemed to offer only one way out: marriage to a certain Captain Danvers.

As the chaos of the day began with William's appearance at breakfast, she strived to block it out, focusing instead on the suffering of those outside the house. The column was a particularly long one, with notices of long lost relatives urgently seeking their family members and lovers conveying the details of their illicit meetings. She came upon the last advertisement and her heart skipped a beat in excitement. Worried she'd misread it, she read it again.

"K. is a strict disciplinarian and not afraid of a rather unruly pupil."

Could it be? Had she found a tutor for William? As she attempted to ignore his stomping and temper tantrum over his mother's timid request he finish his oatmeal, Lily read and reread the notice, her anticipation building at the thought of someone finally disciplining the child properly.

"Elizabeth," she said as he stormed out of the room to abuse the cook, "how would one find a person who advertised in the Agony Column?"

Her sister-in-law looked relieved at the idea of discussing other people's distress. "I don't know for sure, but you would likely have to advertise a reply."

Lily almost leaped from her chair, thrilled by the prospect of hiring William's newest tutor—a strict disciplinarian!

"Elizabeth, please have John arrange the carriage for me. I'm going into town."

As the carriage rolled toward London, the steady rhythm of the horses' hooves hitting the road relaxed Lily. Closing her eyes, she shut out everything but the sound and allowed herself to fantasize about the mysterious stranger she hoped would soon bring calm and order to the house.

My mid-morning she'd placed her reply to the potential tutor and was on her way back home. As her carriage pulled up to the house, she congratulated herself on being such a take charge woman. Her triumph was cut short, however, by the vision of Mason Danvers she spied through the carriage window. Taking a deep breath,

she resigned herself to the fact that what she'd dreaded had begun. As he helped her out of the carriage, she felt his gaze roam over her. Ever the military man, he was surveying the prize he sought to capture and devising a plan of attack, she thought to herself.

"Miss Scott, how are you today?"

Lily immediately felt irritated by his negation of her three years of marriage. Pretending he was a stranger, she asked in an indignant tone that was only partially false, "Do we know each other, sir?" as she haughtily took back her hand.

Bowing, he said, "Pardon me, dear lady. I understand you may not remember me as I do you, but I'm here at your brother's request. I'm Captain Mason Danvers. Please let me escort you into the house."

Lily looked at the man her brother had chosen for her intended. As appealing as she remembered, he appeared to be genuinely interested in her, she realized to her surprise.

"Thank you, Captain. That's very nice of you," she answered more politely than genuinely.

She let him take her hand once more and felt the strength of his hand press gently against her skin. The power he possessed seemed to exude from his very pores, and she decided perhaps she should try to like him.

The problem was just as his every movement seemed to convey a very attractive strength, his speech conveyed a far less attractive overconfidence at times that she found more and more distasteful.

"Richard, I look forward to discussing that business

deal with you. I believe I can help you as much as you may help me."

Lily watched as he strutted into the parlor with her brother. Her first real meeting with Captain Mason Danvers had left her with mixed feelings for him. True, he seemed to have some fine qualities, but as she watched him staring at her from an entire room away, she sensed she was the business deal he'd wanted to discuss.

Well, if he thinks closing this deal will be easy, he's definitely overestimated himself.

Two

"Master Kadar, your newspaper and tea."

Kadar watched as his servant placed a tray containing the items next to him on the small table that stood beside his chair. "Have there been any letters this morning?"

The servant reached into his jacket and retrieved two letters. "These just arrived."

Taking them from him, Kadar excused him with a wave and began reading the first of the two letters. What he found pleased him, and he made a mental note to arrange a meeting with the letter writer in the near future. A quick skim of the second letter produced the same pleasure and another reminder to meet that person also.

After a sip of tea, he opened the newspaper to find out the news of the day. Eventually, he came back to the Agony Column and reading through the brief but tortured listings for that day, his eyes came upon an unexpected ad responding to his own.

"L. is in need of a strict disciplinarian. Please advise to allow a meeting."

His focus was riveted to the words as he read them. Who was L? Quickly, he thought of all the "pupils" he'd hoped to reach with his notice and none possessed a name beginning with the letter L.

"Akil!" he bellowed to the servant, who hurriedly ran into the room in response.

"Yes, Master."

"Did you deliver the exact advertisement I gave you the other day?"

"Yes, Master. The exact one. 'K. is a strict disciplinarian and not afraid of a rather unruly pupil.'"

"Get me yesterday's Times."

As he waited for Akil to return, he wondered who the mysterious L. could be. Known only to a few people in London, he'd used the Agony Column many times before to meet people like him. Always reliable, it had offered him an anonymity he desired but a trustworthy method of reaching out to his kind.

"Here is the paper, Master," the servant said as he nervously handed him the Times of London for May 16, 1853.

Running his finger along the page, he traveled over notes for secret lovers' meetings and ads from those who longed to find estranged loved ones in code and foreign languages. Finally, at the bottom of the column, he saw his advertisement exactly as he'd ordered Akil to submit

it and exactly as his servant had just recited it back to him.

Who was this new "pupil" looking to join the two who'd already responded as he'd expected they would?

"Well, L. wants to meet," he muttered as the servant stood waiting to take the previous day's newspaper.

"Will there be anything else, Master?"

"Yes, Akil," he said as he rose to walk to his desk. When he'd written out a note, he handed it to the man.

"Take this and make sure it's in tomorrow's newspaper. Now hurry and get this to the Times."

Alone again, Kadar sat back in his chair by the window to drink his morning tea and decide on the details of where and when to meet his two letter writers. However, the possibility of a new person looking to join him preoccupied his thoughts, and he began to plan for the meeting he hoped would occur soon.

A new acquaintance would be a welcome, if unexpected, change. He'd advertised to replace the "pupil" he'd lost—in fact, lost would be the wrong word, he thought to himself. He'd willingly given her up when she'd decided to relocate to America, realizing their time together had come to its natural end.

Such was often the case in the world he traveled in. His "pupils" were more often than not curious ladies frustrated with the austere structure of their lives who frequented the underground sex scene. They sought him and others like him out, looking for a way to express what Victorian society hypocritically demanded stay hidden, buried under modest dress, meticulous manners, and a general fear of anything different.

Kadar stood and stretched his muscular frame. While he waited for a response from the mysterious L., he'd keep himself busy with the two who'd answered his advertisement. Summoning his maid, he readied himself for his day.

"Yes, Master?" the petite, dark skinned woman said as she appeared in front of him.

"Prepare my case. I'm going to be spending some time at the country house."

"Yes, Master."

Turning back toward the window, he watched in boredom as his Regent's Park neighborhood began to come alive for the day.

❧

Lily awoke early and hastily dressed, eager to search the newspaper for a response to her ad. She attempted to tamp down her excitement, reminding herself that it had only appeared the day before and it was quite likely that K. was a busy person who may not have answered so quickly.

But she could hope.

As she entered the breakfast room, she was treated to a painful reminder of how desperate she was for K. to agree to her offer. William sat on the floor next to the table obstinately refusing to do as his mother requested until she agreed to take him out.

"Aunty Lily, tell Mother to take me for a ride in the carriage today," he whined.

14

She saw the frustration on her sister-in-law's face and for a moment forgave her for years of poor parenting. Lily pitied her, for as unfortunate as her life had recently been, she could console herself with the idea that at least she wasn't forced to face the result of her shortcomings each day. And as uncertain as her future was, at least she'd leave this house at some point. Elizabeth could look forward to no such reprieve.

Sitting down at the table, Lily casually dismissed his suggestion. "William, your mother has many things to do as the lady of this house. Perhaps if you'd stop misbehaving and chasing away your nannies, you'd get to enjoy trips in the carriage or even time at the park."

Before she'd finished, her nephew had shifted his attention to the cat, which had made the mistake of walking past the doorway. Racing after it, William left the two women in peace, if only for a few moments.

Lily watched Elizabeth sigh deeply, looking far older and more haggard than her twenty-six years. She hoped K. had answered the ad as much for her sister-in-law as for herself.

Opening the paper, she immediately turned to the Agony Column with high expectations. Her eyes flowed over the words until they stopped abruptly at the answer she'd waited for.

"K. instructs his new pupil to appear in blue at the S.E. pavilion in Regent's Park on Thursday noon."

Lily could barely contain her exhilaration. The tutor had seen her notice and wanted to meet his new pupil! In her joy, she heard William stomp his feet at the suggestion he leave the cat alone and let out an ear-piercing scream.

"No! He's my kitty!"

She couldn't take him to meet the tutor or the man would immediately refuse the appointment! In a flash, her joy turned to despair. No tutor, not even one who believed in strict discipline, would ever agree to work with the child if he acted like that.

But the ad had specifically said the pupil was to appear the next day in the park, and Lily knew no manner of cajoling would change William into the kind of child any tutor would agree to teach in just one day. She'd just have to go by herself and hope to convince him to take the position.

Right before noon, Lily reached the southeast pavilion in Regent's Park. The focal point of the London suburb that shared the same name, the park was an oasis from the effects of the city that often spilled over into the carefully planned neighborhood that skirted the capital. On this mid-May day, the sun shone brightly, and she immediately entered the pavilion to avoid getting any unsightly coloring from the sun. Suntans may have been permissible for Army men, but a proper English lady would never allow such a thing.

Lily scanned the area in search of the man she hoped would be her nephew's next tutor and her savior. People walked by, enjoying the pleasant spring day. A rainbow of colored parasols danced against the deep green lawn. She looked down at her blue dress the color of robin's eggs and nervously worried another would wear blue

and steal her tutor out from under her nose, but no one else appeared in any shade of blue nearby, and Lily smiled to herself at her needless concern.

Church bells announced the arrival of noon, and as she listened to the deep chimes, she heard someone enter the pavilion behind her. Turning to face the stranger, she saw a man she identified as a foreigner, probably from Arabia.

"Miss, pardon me. I am sent to give you this note."

Taking it from his hand, she asked, "Are you the person who placed the notice for pupils?"

The man shook his head. "No, miss. All will be answered in the letter."

Lily read the note and looked up to see the man waiting for her response. What had seemed like a simple meeting in the park had quickly become more complicated. K. requested she meet with him at his country home in Hertfordshire.

Propriety should have strictly forbidden her from going any further, but desperation trumped caution and proper etiquette. Lily wrestled briefly with the decision but quickly nodded.

"Please tell your employer I will arrive within the next two hours."

Bowing, the man thanked her and left her standing alone in the pavilion. After steeling herself against the idea that what she was about to do was entirely improper for a young woman, she left to arrange a carriage to take her to Hertfordshire.

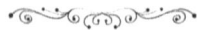
"What did she look like?"

Kadar watched as his servant appeared to carefully consider his reply.

"Very English, Master. Dark hair worn in the style popular with young English ladies. Pale skin but very green eyes."

"Green?"

Akil nodded slowly. "Deep green, like a precious emerald."

"And the rest of her?" Kadar asked, his interest already piqued.

"Very much to your liking, if I am any judge of your preferences."

"And she agreed to meet here?"

"She will be here within the hour, Master."

"Then I will soon meet the mysterious Miss L. Be sure to obtain her full name and inform me before escorting her to the parlor."

"As you wish."

Kadar sat down and tried to relax, but the anticipation of a potential new "pupil" made it next to impossible. As the minutes ticked away, he fantasized about her with the information Akil had provided. While he thought about the pleasure someone new would give him, he spied out the window a figure exiting a coach at the end of the lawn.

Her beauty hit him like a thunderbolt, but immediately something about her looked familiar. He watched as she

walked up the path to the front door and realized with a shock that the woman coming to meet him was one of his Regent's Park neighbors.

"What on earth is Richard Scott's sister doing here?" he muttered in amazement.

A minute later, Akil confirmed what he'd seen outside. "Mrs. Lily Norville is waiting, Master. Shall I show her in?"

Kadar weighed his options and smiled. He'd never known Richard's sister to be anything but the proper English lady she was expected to be, but if she were here to become someone's "pupil", there was obviously more to her than what she appeared to be.

"Show her in, but instruct her to stand with her back to the window. Tell her I refuse to see her if she doesn't follow my explicit instructions."

Akil returned to the hallway to retrieve her, and Kadar slipped behind the decorative screen near the window to wait.

As she entered the room, she untied her bonnet and removed it to reveal beautiful dark brown curls fastened in the fashion of the day. Kadar thought how incredibly sensual it would be when he freed them and her from her restraints.

But other restraints would replace those.

He watched as she dutifully positioned herself as instructed and waited. How trusting she was!

Silently, he moved behind her and before she could protect herself, he had his hands around the column of her neck, his fingers holding her chin and forcing her head to remain facing forward. He felt her tremble in fear as he pressed his body against her back.

"Please don't hurt me," she pleaded in a frightened voice.

Whispering, he said, "That's not what this is about. Force is for brutes and blackguards."

"Then why are you holding me like this?" she asked, her voice shaky.

Kadar brushed his lips against her ear and inhaled the sweet fragrance of her perfume. "You're lovely, my dear."

He felt her body stiffen against his when he kissed the soft skin of her neck, but there was excitement in her too, evidenced by the slight heaving of her breasts and her gentle panting. One hand released her chin and slid down to caress the tops of her milky white breasts.

"Lovely."

As he trailed his fingertips over the skin above her breasts, he felt her push against his hand holding her jaw.

"Eyes forward, my dear," he whispered into her ear.

"There's been some mistake," she began.

"What you want isn't a mistake. You don't have to be frightened. I would never hurt you," he assured her in between gently kissing her neck.

"Please let me go. This is a mistake. I came here for a tutor for my nephew."

Kadar lifted his head from her shoulder and stared at her, stunned at the realization that she'd taken his advertisement literally. She hadn't wanted to experiment as a submissive. She had believed she was meeting a

child's tutor!

Closing his eyes, he inhaled her fragrance one last time, disappointed by the misunderstanding. Just touching her for that brief time had excited him, but he wouldn't force her.

"Take care, my lady," he whispered and then quietly slipped away behind the screen.

Released, she ran for the door and in seconds she was gone, running to her carriage to escape. Watching from the window, he saw her throw herself into the seat and order the driver to leave. She sped away, and he slumped into a chair, still excited but disappointed by the all too brief encounter.

"Too bad," he mumbled to himself.

The ride back to Frederick Street seemed to take twice as long as the ride to Hertfordshire as Lily struggled to understand what had happened. Her fingers caressed the path his lips had taken over her neck, and her face grew warm at the memory of him holding her as he began his seduction.

Emotions that had lay dormant since her husband's death bubbled up inside her. Deep in the pit of her stomach an ache she barely remembered settled into her.

Who was he? Who was the man whose touch had ignited such feelings of desire in her?

Quickly, she chastised herself for such a baseless infatuation. "Whoever he is, he's obviously a man whose tastes run far differently than mine," she said aloud, as if to convince herself. But the feelings he caused in her remained.

For the rest of the day, Lily worked to banish the thoughts of the stranger from her mind. Whatever he was, he wasn't the answer to her problems.

Three

L ily knew as soon as she hit the main floor that her brother had taken the next step toward encouraging a union between her and Captain Danvers. The kitchen staff scurried from stove to counter preparing the finest pheasant and wild herb meal, and the Scott's maid and head man obsessed over seating placements and dinnerware as if the Queen herself was to grace the household.

"Elizabeth, are we to entertain guests?"

"Oh, yes! Richard has invited Captain Danvers, Jeremiah Needham, and his business partner, Joseph Cranston. And their wives, of course. Now you must go back to your room and get ready. The guests will be arriving soon."

Three couples and a single man. Richard wasn't aiming for subtlety, it seemed. It was perfect, wasn't it? Lily saw all too clearly that she was in for an evening of matchmaking. She consoled herself with the fact that at least her brother wasn't arranging an engagement with a man as old as Mr. Needham, who was at least sixty.

"It could be worse," she reassured herself as she climbed the stairs back to her room.

By six o'clock, all the guests had arrived and Lily was enjoying old Jeremiah Needham's stories of his days fighting Napoleon.

"Sir, your tales are some of the most exciting I've ever heard," she said after he'd finished telling of his time at the Battle of Waterloo.

"And they're all true, young lady. Bonaparte was every bit the rascal I make him out to be," the older man boasted.

"Well, thankfully, England had fine soldiers like you ready to give their all to defeat him."

Having flattered and impressed Richard's guests, she deftly moved to find a quiet spot near the front window in the parlor, but found Mason Danvers at her elbow.

"Do you enjoy old Needham's tall tales, Miss Scott?"

Turning to face him, she stared intently into his eyes. "As a widow, Captain Danvers, I still retain the last name of my husband."

Instantly, she saw his face register her offense to his mistake. Something in his eyes telegraphed his regret even before he spoke.

"Please accept my sincerest apologies. I thought it better not to remind you of your sadness."

Lily knew his intent hadn't been to offend and let a smile soften her expression. "Captain Danvers, please

simply call me Lily and all will be forgiven."

All worry left his eyes and at once they seemed to sparkle, gold flecks dancing through the soft brown color. "Then I hope you'll call me Mason. Captain is for old men who try to flirt with young women by telling stories they hope will impress them."

Chuckling, she said, "Mason, I think you're too hard on Mr. Needham."

"I can only hope I don't behave like that when I reach his age."

"Do you have exciting military stories from your time abroad?"

"How do you know I've been abroad, Lily?"

Motioning with her eyes toward the rest of the party, she explained, "Quite simply, you have the look of someone who's seen sunnier regions. Look at my brother, for example. An Englishman if there ever was one. Look at his pale skin. Now look at yourself. It's obvious from your coloring that you've been abroad. Was it India?"

"No. I was in the Afghan wars."

Lily sensed by the darkening in his expression that his days at war weren't something he wanted to discuss and tried to lighten the conversation. "The peace and quiet in the house is quite nice, isn't it?"

Mason looked around the room. "It is indeed. Where is your nephew tonight?"

"Exiled to my sister-in-law's family for the duration of the party."

"He is a spirited one, isn't he?" Mason said with grin.

"You are most kind in your description of him."

"Boys are meant to be spitfires, Lily. That's where our military leaders come from."

"Well, while the military may benefit from his high spiritedness years from now, we would benefit from some better behavior now. In fact, I'm actively looking for a new nanny and tutor for him."

"Any luck finding one?"

Lily's mind momentarily returned to her afternoon adventure. Shaking her head, she said, "No, no luck yet. But I'm not giving up. Our sanity depends on my succeeding in finding someone to discipline the boy."

They heard Elizabeth call then to dinner, and as they returned to the dining room, Lily felt like she'd seen a different, more appealing side to Mason Danvers.

Alone in her bed, she thought of the man's hands, strong yet gentle, holding her exactly where he wanted her that afternoon. The memory of his control over her nagged at her, like an idea that haunted her into thinking something she shouldn't.

Everything about her experience in Hertfordshire should have frightened her so completely as to cause nightmares for days.

But it didn't.

Instead she found herself slipping into a fantasy about the man—the seductive smell of spices that had teased her nose as he dipped his mouth to her neck.

The power in his strong fingers as they controlled her movements.

The husky whisper of his voice in her ear reassuring

her he wouldn't hurt her.

Lily blushed in the darkness as her body came alive, reacting to the pictures her mind conjured up. It had been so long since she'd felt anything for another she'd feared she'd never again respond to a man's touch.

As she lay there, her Victorian propriety scolded her for her wanton thoughts.

"That's not how a lady is supposed to be treated," she told herself. "A gentleman never places a hand on a young woman, unless he's a brute."

Everything she'd been brought up to believe told her to forget the incident and be thankful for escaping without harm. Everything was no match for the feelings he'd stirred in her, however.

But ingrained beliefs refused to leave her so easily, and by the time she began to drift off to sleep, she'd convinced herself that the afternoon's excitement was a memory best forgotten quickly.

By morning, Lily had decided all her energy should be focused in the hiring of the desperately needed nanny and tutor. Attacking her task with a newfound vigor, she scoured the Times, careful to avoid the Agony Column. Luck seemed to be on her side and two potential nannies were her reward.

Feeling flush with the potential for success, she decided she owed it to her brother to keep him abreast of her efforts. As he sat at the head of the breakfast table dreamily looking out the window at the bright spring day, Lily explained what she'd done so far to solve their dilemma.

"Richard? Did you hear me?"

He seemed to come out of his haze at these words and looked at her blankly, obviously unaware of everything she'd said. "I'm sorry. Did you say something?"

"I was explaining that I have two fine leads for a nanny, but I've had no luck so far finding a suitable tutor for William."

A smile slowly formed on his face, but he looked away past her. "Lily, you're going to make a fine mother. I'm sorry Jeremy died before you were blessed with a child."

A tiny stab of sadness hit Lily. "Thank you, Richard."

The two sat in silence until he turned toward her again. "I'd never noticed how noisy this house is until this moment. I guess I'd just gotten used to it."

Reaching her hand out to touch his, she said, "I don't plan to give up until I find William both a nanny and a tutor. Not only for his sake, but for yours and Elizabeth's."

"We're going to miss you when you leave, Lily."

"Have you married me off already?"

"No, but Mason was very impressed with you last night. He told me you two had a thoroughly interesting conversation."

Lily watched as her brother's paternal side took over. She knew he was right: this was a woman's only choice. And as far as men went, Captain Mason Danvers wasn't a bad choice. A little brash, a tad bit bold, but not a bad choice in many ways.

But something deep inside her whispered its desire for something else. Something darker and more foreign

than anything she'd ever experienced in her life.

"Thoroughly interesting?"

As she asked the question, she heard the disdainful tone she'd attached to it. Richard's expression told her he'd heard it too.

"Lily, I don't want you to think I'm trying to get rid of you because I'm encouraging Mason. He's a good man, and he can give a woman a great deal."

Suddenly feeling ungrateful, she lowered her eyes. "I don't feel like you're trying to get rid of me, Richard. I just don't know if he's the kind of man for me."

"He thinks a great deal of you, sister."

Smiling her agreement, she wondered if it mattered at all what she thought of him.

"And he can offer the security and comfort you deserve."

"I know. And I know that you only want the best for me."

Lily listened as he listed all of Mason Danver's assets, all important things people like her brother considered when arranging a match. All his money and prestige meant little to her, though. She'd never been as concerned as all those around her about wealth and social position, much to the chagrin of their parents, who'd hoped to see her married to someone far higher on the social ladder than Jeremy Norville. But he'd always been the one for her from the moment she met him.

Memories of those days made her sad now. She'd had everything she'd ever hoped for and in the blink of an eye, it had all been taken away. What if that happened again? Could she bear caring about Mason, falling in love with him, and then losing him too?

"And after his time abroad, he's ready to settle down and live the life of a proper English gentleman."

Lily nodded her understanding. "I promise I will give him a fair chance, not only for his sake but for yours."

"That's all I ask."

By dinnertime, Lily had great news to tell. One of the nannies had agreed to accept the position and, in fact, possessed the necessary qualities to be William's governess, both nanny and tutor. Everyone looked forward to the new addition to the household, and even William seemed to enjoy the idea.

Days went by and her hopes for Miss Allen proved true. With a caring yet firm hand, she immediately began to affect change in the child, much to the rest of the household's relief. Lily watched as her nephew began to morph from a petulant tyrant of a child to one who still seemed to have a very spirited side but was also capable of being polite and behaved.

William's transformation made life better for the entire Scott household, but Lily couldn't shake the memory of the man who seemed to be causing a change in her. Every night, as she lay in bed wishing for sleep, she was tormented by memories of his touch, his lips on her skin, his powerful presence behind her commanding her to be something she wasn't.

Or was she? As she relived the brief time she'd spent with him, she wanted more. Feelings of need and desire

spiked between her legs as she thought of his long fingers replacing hers on the spot she touched and bringing her an even more exquisite release.

By the eighth day, she was back at the offices of the Times of London with another notice for the Agony Column. Unsure if she was entering a world she would eventually run in fear from, she placed her ad and hoped more than she understood that he would answer with his own beckoning her back to him, for she'd realized after nights full of thoughts of him that she would be in her own agony until she was with him again.

That night, as she lay awake in bed, she fantasized about her own potential tutor. Her delicate fingers caressed her tender thighs, over skin that hadn't felt the touch of another for far too long. The thought of his hands — his mouth — touching her there, excited her like she'd never been before, sending heat racing over her skin. Timidly, she touched her soft folds, imagining his mouth between her legs. Her other hand excitedly squeezed her thigh with each stroke of her excited nub as her mind wandered back to the feel of the man's hands on her, the way he held her so completely in control. She imagined his fingers trailing over her neck as his lips gently teased her earlobe, his voice whispering erotic words of seduction. And domination. Silently, as she felt her orgasm overtake her, she prayed he would call to her soon and show her if her desire was reciprocated.

Four

Kadar sat in the study of his Regent's Park home preparing for his day. As he sipped the very black chai tea his Afghan servant had delivered, he inhaled deeply, enjoying the sweet but spicy scent of the cardamom added to it. His mind traveled back to the world where he'd first experienced the food and drink he now regularly enjoyed. Thoughts of the desert sands and his life there contrasted sharply with his current life in England.

"How different it is here," he mumbled as he sat back in his chair. In England, he was essentially a man of leisure, each day attending appointments with other men like him. There he'd been anything but that type of man.

But one similarity existed between the two very different worlds. Just as in the wilder world of his past, he still enjoyed the underground sexual world of domination and submission. And to his surprise, he'd

found many more willing participants here in England.

Reflecting on his most recent time with a new submissive, he causally thumbed through the newspaper and drank his morning tea. He read through the Agony Column, even though he no longer advertised, because like so many other Londoners he couldn't resist the mystery the column offered in the staid and responsible days of Victoria.

Before he'd made it halfway through, he saw it.

"L. misses her tutor and wishes to resume her studies."

Kadar's heart beat wildly against his chest as he reread the message he knew was meant for him. Lily had drifted in and out of his mind since the day he'd watched her run from his house. He'd accepted, albeit with disappointment, that what he'd hoped for had no chance of occurring. She was a proper society woman through and through.

But as he ran his fingertips over her words, he saw that he'd been mistaken. She was certainly a lady on the surface, but like so many of the women he'd met, she craved something more than the bland sexuality mid-nineteenth century restrictive morals forced her to accept.

No, she's different than those women, he thought to himself as his mind replayed her sweetly innocent response to him as she stood naively in his Hertfordshire home.

Her ad had given little evidence of the passion he suspected he'd find within her. His fantasy of that passion raced through his thoughts, building upon itself with each new desire he conjured.

Just as he believed her passion to be far deeper than the façade of a perfect English lady let on, he also knew he'd have to be patient and gently initiate her into the world she timidly approached. Too much too soon and she'd run.

No, he'd need to take his time.

As he considered how sweet her surrender would be when it finally came, his growing erection pushed against his trousers. His body preferred to move much faster than he should.

A knock at the door roused him from his fantasies, and as his servant entered to refresh his drink, he said, "Akil, I will need you to take another letter to the Times just as before."

The man nodded. "Will there be anything else, Master?"

Kadar rose from his chair to retrieve a pen and paper. When he was finished composing his ad, he handed it to him. "After you deliver this to the paper for tomorrow's edition, I want you to go to the market."

"Yes, Master."

He handed Akil another sheet of paper with a list of items he desired. "Make sure you obtain the ingredients for Qabili Palau. And I want the best chocolates, so go to the confectionary near Hyde Park. Do you know the one I mean?"

Akil smiled a knowing smile and bowed. "I know exactly the one, Master."

"Then go. And when you retrieve everything on that list, take it to Hertfordshire. We'll be going there

tomorrow morning."

"Will there be anything else?"

Kadar thought about his question and quickly scribbled another note. "Have this delivered to the young woman named Violet. And send Nuha in."

Bowing deeply, Akil took the paper and left to begin his errands. With his exit, Kadar's maid and sometimes cook entered the study. She stood quietly waiting for him to give her orders, her gaze directed toward the floor.

When he'd finished writing another note, he looked up at her. "Nuha, you'll be going to Hertfordshire in the morning. I'll need you to cook for a gathering I'll be having tomorrow. I sent Akil to get all the ingredients you'll need for Qabili Palau, and I want you to make baklava."

"Yes, Master. I will require rosewater. Do you prefer I purchase it or make it myself?"

"Do whatever it takes to ensure the baklava tastes like it did when you first made it for me."

"As you wish. I will need roses then."

Handing her money, Kadar instructed her to find Akil to add the flowers to his list. When she'd left, he relaxed at his desk and returned to his fantasy of his next meeting with Lily.

Lily awoke from a night filled with decadent dreams, her entire body humming with excitement. She'd submitted her ad in time for yesterday's paper and anticipated his answer today. Butterflies fluttered in her stomach at seeing something meant especially for her.

Everyone else in the house had finished breakfast, so she was able to search the paper in private. But as she began to read the Agony Column, Mason Danvers was announced and led into the breakfast room.

"Captain Danvers, this is an unexpected surprise," she said with frustration as she folded the Times in her lap.

"Good morning, Lily. It's wonderful to see you again. I'm here to meet with your brother, but I don't see him. Is he here?"

"I'm not sure where he is, but please take a seat and feel free to wait."

"That's very kind of you. Thank you. Please don't let me interrupt you. I saw you were reading the paper as I entered."

"No, that can wait. I wouldn't be much of a hostess if I read the paper while you sit here with me."

Lily accepted that she would have to wait just a short while longer to find out if her mystery man from Hertfordshire had answered. She and Mason conversed about goings on in Regent's Park and William's new nanny until Richard returned for their meeting.

"Thank you for another lovely time, Lily," Mason said as he stood to join her brother.

Smiling, Lily eagerly returned to the newspaper and the Agony Column. Three-quarters of the way down the page she found her answer. As her heart pounded against her chest, she read each of his words with delight.

"K. welcomes his wayward pupil L. at three o'clock at

his home on Saturday."

Instantly, her face felt hot and the flush traveled over her body as she reread the enticing words. He would welcome her that very afternoon!

Looking up, she saw Mason staring at her as he spoke to her brother. Embarrassed, she meekly smiled and was greeted by Mason's full grin, which only served to heighten her discomfort.

Turning away, she looked out the window and tried to calm herself so as not to attract any undue attention. Every cell in her body felt alive as she thought about what may begin in just a few hours. She would finally meet her stranger face to face. The idea of what they'd do afterward made her heart begin to pound again, and her breathing quickly became labored, her breasts gently rising and falling as she closed her eyes to envision the delights that awaited her in Hertfordshire.

Her reverie was broken by Mason's voice. "Are you feeling all right, Lily?"

Confused and flustered, she turned to see him standing near her. Quickly, she closed the paper to conceal the source of her excitement.

"Yes, yes. I'm fine. Thank you."

"Did you read something in the paper that upset you? It seems like every day the news becomes more filled with the depravity so many in our fine city wallow in."

"No, I'm fine."

Was what she planned to do that afternoon depraved? Just months before, she may have answered yes with little doubt, but now she was far less assured of her answer.

Nothing had ever excited her as much as the feel of the man's hands controlling her.

Standing from the table, she hastily excused herself, leaving the men to continue their discussion. Alone in her room, she excitedly prepared for her journey to Hertfordshire, unsure of everything but her desire to see the man again.

It was nearly three o'clock as her coach rambled to the designated meeting place. Lily fought back the urge to instruct the driver to turn around and return to the safety of her brother's home on Frederick Street. Twice before on the trip, she'd almost lost her nerve, fearing what she was about to do. But just as she had in those moments of doubt, she once again steadied herself and admitted that she wanted this, no matter what society would think.

She'd worn her most flattering dress, a pale pink that flattered her more than any others she owned. Nervously, she fixed the stray curls that had escaped her bonnet, wishing she possessed hair that behaved as it should.

Exiting the carriage, she looked around but saw no one. The country home of K. was thankfully private she noted as she approached the front door. Her knock was answered by the same man who'd greeted her on her first visit, and just as before, he showed her into the room and instructed her to wait with her back to the window. As she stood waiting for the stranger to come up behind her, Lily was sure she'd never been as excited in her entire life as she was in these moments anticipating his first touch. When he finally ended her tortured wait, she reacted

with a start.

Gently, his hands held her head so she remained eyes forward, and his words reassured her. "There's no need for fear. I would never hurt you, Lily."

The way he spoke her name sounded like a secret whispered only to her. It thrilled her, and instantly she felt her nipples harden into tightened pearls pressing against the fabric covering them.

He began his sweet assault on her neck, planting kisses in a path from her ear to her collarbone as he held her fast with his hand on her jaw. Gradually, the flick of his tongue was added to his kisses, exciting her even more. Lily was powerless to stop a small moan from escaping from her throat when he spoke again.

"You are so lovely, my pupil."

Before she could think of what to say, his body moved away from behind her, only his hand left touching her as he held her chin firmly. When he returned, she felt the warmth of his body press against hers and his free hand held something in front of her face.

"Lily, I want you to wear this whenever we're together. You may refuse, but if you do, there will be no more meetings."

Each word on its own was said in a purely seductive whisper, but the meaning of them together unnerved her. Would she never see him? And why was she forbidden from seeing his face?

For a long moment he remained still, as if waiting for her answer. When she quietly acquiesced, he positioned the blue silk blindfold over her eyes and fastened it in a tie behind her head. Then he released her face and moved away from her once again.

Immediately frightened by her newfound helplessness, she lifted her hands in defense to feel for safety in front of her.

"Don't be frightened. I'm right here," he said as he slowly pulled her to him, pressing his broad chest against her gently heaving breasts.

Lily waited in sweet anticipation for him to begin his assault on her mouth, eager to finally kiss him with all the desire inside her, but instead he only very softly brushed his lips against hers, increasing her need.

Parting her lips to encourage him to intensify his kiss, she felt his soft breath as he whispered "lovely" against her mouth before pulling away. Lily pressed her lips together and bit her lower lip in frustration. How much she wanted to feel his lips on hers, devouring her passion and giving her his!

"I have something for you."

He took her by the hand and led her away from the window. After only a few steps, he stopped her and gently eased her down to the floor. Unaccustomed to sitting this way, she began fidgeting and smoothing the front of her dress.

"Don't move. And no fidgeting," he quietly commanded.

She heard his footsteps move away from her but was unsure if he left the room when he opened the door. She sat still as a statue but fearful of what he had for her. Was it a gift, she wondered as she sat waiting for what could bring her pleasure or pain?

Five

The door closed and a mixture of aromas wafted across the room. Sweet and spicy smells filled her nose, along with other fragrances she couldn't place at first. The variety was pleasantly overwhelming, and she breathed in deeply trying experience each of them.

She sensed him sitting in front of her, but she remained still as he'd ordered. Her fear had faded, and now she waited for him to hand her a plate and fork to eat the delicious food he'd kindly prepared for her.

"Lily, have you ever been fed by a man who wants to make love to you?"

The effect of his frank words left her speechless, and she merely shook her head. Was he going to feed her before they made love? Just the thought of it was more erotic than anything she'd ever heard of, let alone done.

"Open your mouth," he said in his softly commanding

tone that made her wish they were already finished with the meal and moved on to what was to follow.

She obeyed and tasted something sweet on her tongue. A wedge of orange exploded juice into her mouth as she bit into it. When she'd finished, his lips pressed against hers, and he kissed her, slipping his tongue into her mouth and tasting the remaining juice from the fruit.

As he pulled away, he whispered against her lips, "Delicious."

She heard him open something, possibly a jar, and then he returned to her and ordered her to open her mouth again. When she did, he stuck his finger in and she closed her lips to suck sweet honey from it. Never before had honey tasted so incredibly good! Aroused, she playfully flicked her tongue against his fingertip as he slowly withdrew his cleaned finger.

Lily licked her lips and waited for the next taste she'd experience, but as she sat there, she realized she'd never learned the name of the man who was feeding her and soon would be inside her.

"What's your name?"

She heard him stop what he was doing next to her, and for a tense moment, she worried she'd done something wrong by asking.

"I'm sorry. I didn't mean to..." she began, but let her voice trail off when she felt his lips brush the shell of her ear and his hand encircle her neck.

"Kadar."

As his hand glided down her neck to rest on her collarbone, she said, "Kadar," repeating his name as if to

seal it in her memory.

Again, he kissed her, his tongue sensually gliding over hers and tasting the sweetness he'd just given her. His kiss, long and passionate, tasted better than any food she'd ever eaten.

He pulled away too soon, and she wished he would end his feeding her and proceed to making love to her. When he began to speak again, she sensed he saw the disappointment on her face.

"When a man truly makes love to a woman, it's more than just thrusting his cock in and out of her, Lily. To truly make love to her, he needs to show her he can take care of her every need."

As he spoke, his fingers lightly caressed her cheek below the blindfold. Leaning in to kiss her, he reassured her, "When I finally make love to you, every other need will have been met."

Lily wasn't sure how much more she could handle. Every touch, every kiss increased her arousal, as evidenced by the growing dampness between her legs. She was glad for a respite when he began asking her questions about herself.

"Tell me about your life, Lily."

Hesitantly at first, she began to explain how she's been married young but happily for just a few short years before her husband was taken by cholera. Overcome by emotion, both from memories of Jeremy and the sweet assault on her senses by Kadar, she began to cry.

"I'm sorry. I should be past crying by now," she said as she lowered her chin to her chest. She may not have been able to see him, but she was sure he was watching her and she didn't want him to see her face.

Silently, he lifted her chin and forced her to face him. Then, very tenderly, he kissed where her tears had fallen on her cheeks but said nothing about her sadness.

"Drink," he ordered as he put a china cup to her lips and tipped it toward her. Slowly, she tasted a very strong tea and its warmth as it flowed down her throat eased her.

"Thank you. That's quite delicious. What kind of tea is it?"

"Chai. It's served black with cardamom. Did you taste that?"

"I thought it was cinnamon."

"No, cardamom is sweeter with a spiciness. Like many great things, it's a mixture of danger and comfort. Like the love I intend to give you."

Lily's eyes grew wide behind the blindfold. So now they'd move on to the lovemaking like she'd had with Jeremy. But his description of love sounded nothing like what she'd done as a wife. There'd been no danger of any sort then.

Tensing, she waited for him to begin, almost afraid of the danger he'd mentioned but desperate for him to ease the ache inside her. But instead of undressing her, she felt his fingers at her mouth ready to feed her again.

"What I'm feeding you now is called Qabili Palau. It's raisins, carrots, and lamb with brown rice. Let it sit on your tongue a few moments before you begin chewing."

Lily did as he said and let the flavors of each ingredient

dance over her taste buds before she finished the helping he'd given her. Each individual taste exploded into her mouth in a mixture just as delicious as the previous flavors but distinctly foreign tasting.

"Did I taste pistachio nuts in that too?"

"Very good. You're quickly becoming my best pupil."

His words brought her back to the reality she should have known but hadn't fully admitted. She was likely one of many women he had. One of many women he treated like this. And not special at all.

She didn't attempt to hide the unhappiness she felt at his words and merely answered, "Oh."

"What's wrong with my Lily?" he asked as he ran his fingers over her pouting lips.

What could she say? That it bothered her that what had been the single most erotic experience of her life was likely commonplace to him? That she was embarrassed that she'd been so naive as to believe he thought of her as she thought of him?

"Do you do this often?" she finally asked.

The pain of hearing the silly plea in her voice was matched by that of the silence that met her question. How foolish she had been to return to him!

Kadar traced the outline of her lips and in a voice that couldn't have more perfect, said, "Whatever I've done or whomever I've done it with, it wasn't like this or with anyone as special."

Lily had never felt as wonderful as she did at that moment. When he fed her another helping of Qabili Palau, she made sure to kiss his fingertips before he moved his hand, for he had said exactly what she'd hoped to hear.

After he'd finished giving her the main entree, Kadar sat silently and Lily wondered if something had happened to change the mood. Before she could ask, he said, "What made you change your mind, Lily?"

After a long moment, she admitted, "I couldn't stop thinking of how it felt when you touched me. How you were so powerful."

"Is that what you want? A man to take control? To dominate?"

Even the way he asked it sounded delicious, and Lily closed her eyes to imagine his strong hands on her as he dominated her. But all this was so new to her. Would he force her to do things she couldn't? He'd said force was for brutes when he'd first touched her. Would he still abide by that when they moved past mere touching?

In a voice as unsure as she was, Lily answered. "Yes."

He touched her hair, wrapping his finger around a stray curl. "When you're sure, I promise to give you what you want. But for now, I want to give you something else."

Parting her lips slightly, she felt something like a pastry enter her mouth, and she slowly chewed the delicious dessert, savoring each bite.

"Kadar, what is it? It's wonderful. I'd love some more."

Feeding her another piece, he explained, "It's called baklava. It's made with honey, dough, rosewater, sugar..."

"And pistachios!" she said excitedly.

She heard the smile in his voice when he told her she was correct. Then he pressed his lips to her ear and whispered the words that nearly made her melt inside. "I promise not to do this or anything else with anyone else if you promise to return to me."

The feel of his warm breath on her skin was as arousing as his feeding her and then promising he'd only be with her. She prayed he'd give her some release from the need that was becoming difficult to manage.

"Yes. Please..."

"Please what, my Lily?"

Unable to tell him what she desired, she merely whimpered as he ran his hand up her neck to her chin. For a long moment, he held her silently, and she knew he was staring at her. Then as if something had switched off in him, he moved away from her, leaving her lonely and cold.

"Time to go, Lily. Take my hand."

Confused and her feelings a little hurt, she held his hand as he helped her to her feet. Almost too weak from unmet need, she stood on shaky legs as he guided her back to her place near the window.

Standing behind her, he whispered in her ear, "After I'm gone, take off the blindfold and place in on the chair. Your bonnet is near the door."

"Kadar..."

"I promise when you're sure, I will give you everything you want."

"Please kiss me," she pleaded.

From behind her, he moved to stand facing her and

bent down to gently place a kiss on her lips. So controlled, his lips barely brushed hers, but she wanted more—needed more. Arching up to press her mouth against his, she urged him to intensify the kiss, and their tongues moved passionately together. Lily pressed her body to his and let him feel her excitement. Her breasts pushed against his strong chest, the closeness only increasing her passion. In her desire, she reached up to encircle his neck, but he caught her by the wrists and held her tightly.

"Time to go. Come back Monday at one."

As she began to respond, he moved away from her and vanished, leaving her to remove the blindfold and leave on her own.

Six

Kadar watched as Lily left, disoriented and confused by the abrupt end of their rendezvous. Her taste remained on his lips, and he licked them hoping to have just a bit more of her with him before all he had left were memories. The tightness in the pit of his stomach from the effect she created in him remained, evidenced by his swollen cock pressing against the front of his trousers.

He'd wanted her more than he'd ever wanted a woman. Seated in his chair, he stretched to release the tension of unfulfilled need. Closing his eyes, he let the memory of Lily take him over.

A knock at the door interrupted him, and he was forced back to reality as Akil joined him.

"Yes?"

"Master, will we be staying here or returning to the city?"

"I'll be returning to London for a day, so I'll need you to accompany me. Nuha can return and stay. I'll need to be back here for Monday."

"Yes, Master. Will you need anything additional for that meeting with Mrs. Norville?"

Kadar arched one eyebrow. "Were you eavesdropping at the door, Akil?"

The servant grinned. "No. I simply assumed your return to this house would be because of another meeting with this new lady."

Remembering his promise to Lily, Kadar said, "Only lady from this time on."

"Yes, Master. Does this mean you will need something special for Monday?"

"The velvet ropes."

Bowing, Akil left after he was excused and Kadar sat regretting his inability to daydream about his time with Lily before setting off on his trip back to the city.

⁂

By the time she arrived back home, Lily had run the gamut of emotions. Frustrated as she left Hertfordshire, she'd angrily pledged never to return to Kadar again. By the time her carriage had reached the halfway point of the trip, she had reconsidered her prior decision, thinking herself rash, and had pledged to return when he'd ordered.

But her basic levelheadedness won out over her extreme emotions so that by the time her carriage arrived at Frederick Street, she'd acknowledged Kadar's effect on

her body and soul but restrained her feelings enough to face her family.

As she entered the house, she stopped to listen to the newfound calm William's governess had created. In the parlor, he played with a puzzle quietly as Miss Allen looked on with a watchful eye.

"Aunty Lily, come look at my puzzle! Can you tell what it will be?"

Lily crouched down to examine what looked like a picture of a giraffe on the African plains. Teasing him, she answered, "Is it a hippopotamus?"

"No!" he cried with a squeal. "Guess again."

Pretending to examine it more carefully, she stared at the obvious neck of a giraffe and said, "Is it a squirrel?"

Both William and the governess laughed. "Aunty Lily, you don't know much about animals, do you?"

Chuckling, Lily shook her head. "I guess not. But do you know what I do know about? Wonderful nephews."

Leaning in, she kissed the top of his head and pulled back to tap him gently on the nose.

"What's that smell? It smells like something delicious. Did you bring me a treat?"

Lily recalled how delicious Kadar's baklava had tasted and for a moment became lost in the memory of him feeding her.

"No, but I promise next time to bring you some."

Walking into the dining room, she found Elizabeth arranging the table. Instantly, Lily hoped she wasn't going to have to attend another dinner party. Her emotions were under control for the moment, but she couldn't predict what would happen if she had to pretend to be carefree and sweet after what she'd experienced with Kadar.

"Elizabeth, you aren't entertaining again, are you?"

"Heavens, no! This is simply for us."

Relieved, Lily turned to retreat to her room.

"Lily, there's a letter for you in the hallway."

Her heart leaping in her chest, Lily wondered if Kadar had sent her a message. She quickly walked to the hallway table, anticipating what might be waiting for her. *Is it possible he knows where I live?* She knew she'd told his servant her name, but had she given him her address?

Opening the letter, she saw it was from Mason and relief quickly turned to disappointment. Of course Kadar hadn't sent anything. How silly of her to think he would!

The letter formally requested a carriage ride the next day with Mason, and as much as she was sure it would at the very least be pleasant, she knew she had little reason to decline. As Richard had said, he was a good man.

The next day came all too quickly for Lily, and at one o'clock, Mason promptly arrived for their official first date. Lily knew she should simply be thankful that an eligible man was interested in her. At almost twenty-three, she was no young girl and every day she spent as the widowed sister of Richard Scott instead of the fiancé of some gentleman, her chances of securing the blessing of a second marriage grew slimmer.

Not that she believed any of that. More and more in the recent days she'd become less the proper English lady she'd always believed herself to be. But what she was changing into she didn't know.

Mason took her hand to help her into the carriage and she felt his strength press into her hand. He truly was a fine man, and as she opened up her parasol to shield herself from the midday sun, she slyly studied him.

"Lily, the afternoon is yours. Wherever you'd like to go, your wish is my command."

"Surprise me, Mason."

"Very well. And while I do that, I hope we may get to know one another better."

For almost an hour, Lily and Mason enjoyed a beautiful spring day and the sweet conversation that's found between two souls at the brink of romance. For Lily's part, she began to find many appealing parts to the captain's personality and the recent events with Kadar slipped into the recesses of her mind.

Leaning toward the far side of the carriage, Mason uncovered a box of fine chocolates, each beautifully wrapped in its individual special foil. "Please, let us enjoy a chocolate. They're handmade from the finest confectioner in town."

Lily took a candy and eagerly unwrapped it to find a milk chocolate and almond treat. Placing it on her tongue, all the wonderful feelings she'd experienced the day before with Kadar came flooding back, and she closed her eyes, afraid if she met Mason's gaze he'd see she was far different than the proper lady he believed her to be.

"Do you like it?" she heard him say in a voice that sounded very far away.

Opening her eyes, she turned to face him and smiled. "Yes, very much. Thank you, Mason."

His smile in response reached all the way to his eyes, and her attention was drawn to their warm brown color. In the sun, it seemed like golden flecks swam in the deeper color, creating a very handsome effect. She couldn't help but think he was a very attractive man.

"What kind did you get?" he asked.

"Almond and milk chocolate."

"Oh. I prefer pistachios to almonds, I think."

"Do you?" she asked, pleased to find something they had in common. "I do too. But they're difficult to find, even in our empire's great capital."

"I know. I had them often when I was in Afghanistan. There the natives use them in many dishes, often as a topping."

"Do they? That sounds wonderful."

A long silence grew between them, and Lily was conscious of Mason staring at her. Suddenly uncomfortable, she let her gaze fall to her folded hands in her lap.

"Lily? Is something wrong?"

Her gaze fixed on her lap, she shook her head. She couldn't explain that just the mere mention of pistachios had made her think of another man, a man she'd never seen and who she intended on allowing to do things to her most would denounce as depraved.

"I hope you know I'm very fixed on you."

"Fixed?"

"Yes," he said with a broad smile. "I like you a great deal, Lily."

Feeling her face grow flush, she inwardly found

amusement that his innocent words could make her blush after what she'd done in the past week.

"I'm sure you know I look forward to a time when you'll agree to be my wife."

As he spoke, he gently placed a hand on hers.

"I'm flattered Mason. And please know I think highly of you. I just don't know if I'm ready to marry again."

Lily knew in her heart this wasn't entirely true. Despite not even knowing what Kadar looked like, she knew no man, not even her dear Jeremy, had ignited feelings in her like the ones she experienced when he was near. Kadar she would be ready to marry.

Mason lightly squeezed her hand and nodded. "I'm willing to wait until you're ready, Lily. I'm a patient man who understands that good things in this world often require waiting. And you are very much a good thing."

As she thanked him, she wondered if she was, in fact, such a good thing as she spent the afternoon with one man while thoughts of another delighted her mind.

Seven

onday morning seemed to drag on indeterminably and as the minutes slowly crept by, Lily's anticipation grew and her fear lessened. In mere hours, she would be in Hertfordshire again with the man who lately took up more of her thoughts than any other person in her life.

Would he feed her sweet delights and foreign treats as he had two days ago? Would they make love, his strong hands possessing her as they did in the fantasies she rejoiced in nightly? Would he take her to even more fantastic and sensual heights than he had simply with his drugging kisses?

The wait finally over, she left shortly before noon to insure she wouldn't be late. Just as each time before, her trip to Kadar's house was made all the more thrilling by the mystery of what she would find there.

She'd specially chosen a blue dress, believing blue to

be his favorite color, and her most flattering white bonnet, which she hoped highlighted her brown hair. Everything had to be perfect.

It was enough for him to like her. She wanted him to feel for her what she now felt for him. She wanted him to think about her every day, wishing she were near him, wanting her kiss—her touch—more than anything else. Needing them more than anything else.

"Akil, I want you to show my guest to the usual room."

The servant looked up from what he was doing and his expression showed his confusion. "Not your bedroom, Master?"

Kadar let a slow smile settle into his features. "Not yet."

Bowing his head in obedience, the servant resumed his chores silently as Kadar delicately fingered the black velvet ropes, twisting them around his hands and wrists.

As Akil made his way out of his master's study, Kadar added, "And I want you to make sure there are pistachios in the room. Nuha had some for the baklava, so find them."

"Yes, Master."

Alone, Kadar's excitement grew as he waited for her to arrive. This time, now that he'd begun to earn her trust, he'd move her closer to submission.

He brought the ropes to his lips, kissing them as he imagined them around her delicate, white wrists, just tightly enough to restrain her but never hurting her.

The sound of her carriage arriving drifted in through the open window, and Kadar moved to watch her approach his home. She looked so sweetly innocent in her pale blue dress and white bonnet.

Concealing himself from her view, he watched as her deep green eyes, wide with eager excitement, studied his home's façade. How he wished to kiss her after gazing lovingly into those eyes! Soon....

In the short time since she'd entered his life, she'd became almost all he thought of, day and night. She'd enchanted him as no other woman on any continent had ever done, and he hadn't even made love to her yet. But his desires leaned in ways other than simple lovemaking. Would she agree and ultimately submit to his unique proclivities? Or would fear of the unknown stop her before he could show her the sensual delights he preferred?

From behind the screen, he watched her carefully position herself just as she knew to, back to the window and eyes forward as she waited. Carefully, she removed her bonnet and tucked stray curls into place. Something in her movements seemed so sweet and his body tensed, stopping him. For a moment he questioned if he should continue taking her to that place of pain and pleasure. Almost as if a sign to let him know the answer, he heard her whisper his name.

"Kadar, I'm here."

He silently approached her, already almost overcome by the desire to have her, and as before, encircled her neck with his one hand as the other held her face forward.

"My Lily," he whispered as he pressed his lips to her neck.

The way she leaned back toward him, melding to his body, told him she yearned for him as he did her.

Swallowing hard against his hand, she said in a shaky voice, "I missed you."

The statement seemed unfinished, as if she'd wanted to say more but was too timid.

Kadar ran his hand up the front of her neck to join the hand holding her jaw. "Are you ready for your blindfold?"

Her voice still shaky, she nodded and answered. "Yes."

He ensured her blindfold fit snugly and stood in front of her watching as she tentatively sought him out. When she found him nowhere close, she formed her mouth into the adorable pout he loved.

"Come to me, Lily."

Hands forward, she walked toward him until her fingertips touched his broad chest and she pressed her body to his. Looking down at her, he waited for her to present her upturned face to him to kiss.

He held her face in his hands and bent his mouth to hers, deliberately pausing just inches from her. He'd thought of little else than this meeting but reminded himself that he needed to go slowly so as not to frighten her. Today would ensure she trusted him if he proceeded with the utmost care.

"Lily," he whispered against her lips barely touching them.

In her desire, she craned her neck, desperate for the kiss he knew she waited for. Unable to deny her any longer, he greedily took her mouth, running his tongue over hers. Her lips urged him on to satisfy her need, and he began to lose himself in the warmth of her. A quiet moan passed between her lips and he took it inside him, like a pledge she offered.

Before she could try to wrap her arms around his neck, he broke off the kiss and pulled out the ropes. He placed them in her hands, and confused, she dipped her head as if to look at what he'd just given her.

Tenderly stroking her check, he asked, "Have you ever been tied up?"

As the velvet ropes sat in her trembling hands, she silently shook her head. He had to carefully introduce restraints or he'd risk losing her right here.

"Follow me," he ordered as he began to back up toward the couch. As he sat, she remained standing in front of him.

"Turn around, Lily."

Lily rotated for him and returned to face him.

"You look beautiful. Blue is my favorite color."

Smiling broadly, she fidgeted over her dress, smoothing it from the waist. "Thank you! I'm so happy you like it."

Her words were met with silence. Kadar sat back on the couch and gazed up at the innocent creature in front of him. Now it would begin.

Standing up, he kissed her lips softly and quietly announced, "I want to see what you are under this pretty

blue dress."

He saw her stiffen in fear and whispered, "I would never hurt you, Lily. Trust me."

"I do," she said softly.

Kadar made swift work of her dress and undergarments and in seconds Lily stood before him naked. His breath caught in his chest, and he had to restrain himself from opening his trousers and pulling her down on his lap to bury himself as deeply as possible inside her.

Astonished by her beauty, he muttered "lovely" as he softly kissed her, explaining, "I'm going to bind your wrists together. Hold your arms out in front of you."

Taking the ropes from her, he expertly wrapped them around her wrists, making sure she wasn't hurt. Restrained, she was forbidden from holding him.

Slowly, he lowered himself to sit on the edge of the couch and pulled her to him. Unable to hold back any longer, he took a nipple in his mouth and gently sucked, feeling the tender skin harden into a peaked point against the flick of his tongue.

Pulling away, he looked up into her face now full of desire. "Beautiful Lily."

He moved to the other one and began giving his attention to it, eliciting a soft moan from her. Just as with the other nipple, it grew hard in his mouth and he tenderly fastened his teeth to bite down, knowing he had to take care not to frighten her.

Cupping her full breast, he latched on and softly bit her nipple as he gently squeezed the supple skin around it.

"Ow!"

Looking up, he saw a frown on her face. "What did you say?"

"That hurt, Kadar."

He slowly stood and stroked her face. "You told me you wanted to submit to me, Lily. Do you?"

Nodding, she bit her lower lip nervously, and he knew she feared she'd done something to displease him.

"It's all right. But you will have to be punished now."

Instantly, he saw a look of terror cross her features. How wide her beautiful green eyes must have been when she heard she was to be punished!

"Please, no, Kadar."

Cradling her face in his hands, he felt emotion tug at him. Most of the time when he announced to a woman that he intended to punish her, he had to fight to ensure he was seated before they flung themselves across his lap. Lily simply stood trembling in front of him.

"I promise it won't hurt for long, love."

Reaching down behind her, he ran his hand over one cheek, then the other, loving how full and firm they felt under his palm. Then he drew back his hand and let it land with a hard slap on her skin.

Kadar held her upright as the shock of his slap wore off, leaving only the warmth growing where his hand had landed. Although he couldn't see her eyes, he was sure tears began to well up in them.

Gently, he rubbed his hand over the skin, soothing her. "See? Not so bad."

"That hurt!"

Again, he pulled back his hand and smacked her skin just as loudly. He knew she wanted to fight as every muscle in her body tensed, but with her wrists bound and his arm holding her, all she could do was bury her face in his chest and whimper.

He soothed her skin with the hand that had just reddened it, whispering, "Someday you'll ask for this, my Lily."

"Never!"

Holding her to him, he began to repeatedly spank her, ignoring her soft cries and pleas to stop. Each time he inflicted pain, he followed it with the loving caresses she needed to know he cared. Slowly, she stopped protesting and pressed next to his body, grasping at his shirt to find the closeness she craved.

Finally, she reached up to kiss him, aroused by the sensations he was inflicting on her. Unable to hold him, she tugged desperately at his shirt to bring his mouth to hers.

Kadar let her devour his mouth as she pressed against his swollen cock, grinding against it with her moist cunt. She was reacting just as he'd hoped — even more so, to his surprise. She was opening for him, her body begging his to fill her.

But he wasn't ready for that yet. Her body may desire him, but her mind still didn't trust him. He needed her body to convince her mind, and that wouldn't happen if he took advantage and merely fucked her.

He stopped the spanking knowing that one or two more would send her over the edge, and he wanted to prolong this moment. Gently, he stroked her skin with his hand, easing the sting out.

"That's my Lily," he cooed in her ear.

"Please, Kadar," she begged.

"How quickly someday has come," he teased.

She was so responsive that he didn't want to stop. But he could give her what she wanted and still be in control. Sitting on the couch, he guided her onto his lap.

"Sit on top of me, legs apart."

She did as he commanded and positioned herself on his legs, straddling him. His hands glided up and down her sides and over her back, carefully avoiding her still pinkened cheeks.

Just as she became relaxed, he landed his palm on her warmed skin, harder than before. She didn't cry out or plead for him to stop but returned to kissing him, her mouth desperate to express her need. Sure she was close, he caressed her and then slapped her skin one last time.

Then he waited.

His hand tenderly rubbed the skin and he slid a finger between her pinkened globes. Her body tensed and her lips began to tremble against his. Moaning into his mouth, her release began to take over. Her body sought his as she pushed her pulsating clit against his hard cock to extend the sensations he'd created in her.

Her reaction was one of surprise. "Don't fight it, Lily. Let it take you," he said as he pulled her to him and encouraged her to ride him.

God, he wished at that moment he was deep inside her feeling her body milk him to his own climax! He

watched as her beautiful body was wracked by shock after shock from her release.

Up and down she slid over his cock, still covered by fabric, until his pants were drenched from her. She gave in to her abandon so completely, and he urged her body on, squeezing her breasts as she came.

"Kadar...please...yes..."she cried over and over.

Her pleas excited him more, and it took everything in him to not strip off his own clothing and make love to her at that moment, making her come again and again. Her climax receding, she slowed her body against his, making long, slow strokes against his cock

That he'd given her what was likely her first climax without being inside her or enjoying her with his mouth made it all the better. Holding her as she slumped against him exhausted, he waited until she stopped softly panting.

"How's my Lily feel now?"

Her head buried in the crook of his neck, she moaned her answer. "Perfect."

"Would you like to lie down?"

"Is it....was I okay?"

"You were perfect. Open, responsive, sensual. What every man secretly desires."

"Is that what you want?" she asked as she kissed the skin near his collarbone. "Is that what the others are like?"

He stroked her hair knowing she was looking for reassurance. He wanted to give it to her. "I have no others now that I have you. And you're exactly what I want."

Her sigh told him he'd succeeded in showing her how much he cared. But had he succeeded in fully gaining her trust? That he wouldn't know until their next meeting.

"I think it's time you left. Your family will wonder where you are."

Nuzzling his neck, she pleaded, "Please don't make me leave, Kadar. Not yet."

Her voice touched him and he relented, silently wishing neither one of them would be forced to leave the other.

"Very well. For this, you can be the master."

He let her doze on his chest for almost an hour before waking her. The feel of her naked body pressed against his enthralled him, and as he listened to her sleep, he wondered if she would ever truly accept him for longer than a few hours in the afternoon.

After he dressed her, he sat next to her on the couch feeding her pistachios. Still blindfolded, she asked, "Why do you feed me?"

Placing a nut in her mouth, he explained, "I told you that for a man to truly make love to a woman, he needs to show her he can satisfy her every need. I feed you because that's how I can ensure you're not hungry."

"You don't have to do that."

"Yes, I do."

They sat in silence for a few minutes and then he asked, "Would you like me to tell you what I fantasize about when I think of you?"

Almost shyly, she answered, "Yes. Please tell me."

"I imagine lying back naked with you between my

legs and my arms around you as I feed you baklava. We've just made love and I've been inside you for so long you feel as though a part of you is missing when I leave your body."

"How I wish that could be!"

They both fell silent and then Lily asked him a question that caught him by surprise. "Do you make me wear this blindfold because there's something wrong with your face?"

"No."

"Well, you wouldn't have to." Dropping her head, she quietly added, "I'd love you no matter how you look."

Kadar was stunned by her admission and said nothing, which he knew made her uncomfortable as he watched her begin to fidget.

"It's time for you to go, Lily. Come back on Thursday."

She stood and silently let him lead her back to her spot near the window. As he untied her wrists, he kissed each of them and then her lips.

"Your bonnet is on the table. That's where you can leave your blindfold."

Kadar moved behind her and gently wrapped his hands around her slender neck. Leaning in to kiss her behind the ear, he whispered, "Next time I'll show you how much I love you, my Lily," and slipped behind the screen to watch her leave, already missing her.

Eight

Lily closed her eyes as the carriage slowly made its way back home. She replayed every moment of her time with Kadar that day, relishing the memory of each touch of his hands on her body. Never before had a man treated her as he had. Everything about him, so sensual and different, delighted her.

She adjusted her position as the carriage rambled its way over bumpy country roads. Her bottom still stung from his spanking, and each bounce of the carriage seemed to be a renewed assault on her body, without the exquisite sensations his had produced.

What had been fearful at first had quickly transformed into pleasurable, so much so that she'd silently prayed for him to continue his sweet attack on her. Each slap had increased her desire, and each caress afterward only made her more aroused. The sweetly potent combination of pain and comfort had made her want him more than

she'd ever thought possible.

Everything Kadar had introduced to her increased her love for him. Not even Jeremy had made her feel as he did. When she was with Kadar, every part of her felt alive, like she'd awakened from a lifetime spent in a numbed daze, finally able to feel and experience life so acutely.

The reality of her life meant soon the sensations she craved would go unfulfilled, subordinated to a life her brother and society would impose upon her. She would be a proper wife again, the epitome of Victorian grace and manners.

But would she ever truly be able to be that person again after her time with Kadar?

Lily began to despair at the idea of life without him. He'd become central to her happiness. How could she leave behind everything he was for any other man?

Perhaps Kadar could marry her. The thought of spending the rest of her life with him delighted Lily. As the carriage entered the city, she sat daydreaming out the window of a life as Kadar's wife and the sensual joys he'd introduce to her.

Lily's fingers traced the outline across her cheeks where her blindfold lay earlier and closed her eyes to remember the feel of Kadar's palm landing on her delicate skin. Never before had anything like that excited her. She felt herself run wet just thinking of his effect on her.

Lost in her memories, she leaned back against the seat and let her fantasies take her away to places where Kadar was hers and she was his. And the sexual part of her was able to be free.

"Mrs. Norville?"

Lily's eyes flew open to see the driver standing outside the carriage and peering in at her.

"Yes?"

"Is everything all right? We've arrived back home."

"Yes, thank you," she stammered.

Straightening in the seat, Lily gathered herself and moved to exit the carriage. As the driver opened the door, she looked up to see Mason standing on the sidewalk.

"Lily, how are you this afternoon?"

Her bottom still tender, she gingerly exited the carriage with his help.

"Very well, Mason. And you?"

"Delighted to see you again." As he spoke, he gentlemanly offered his arm to escort her into the house.

Taking it, Lily smiled and said thank you. This was to be her life from now on, and she had to accept it. Full of restraint and manners, Mason would make a suitable husband to her suitable wife.

It was all so...suitable.

Nothing she did, nothing she felt with Kadar was suitable.

"Captain Danvers, do you ever crave more excitement than what Regent's Park has to offer?"

Mason smiled and for the briefest of moments, Lily thought she saw a look of something resembling satisfaction in his eyes.

"I'm afraid I've no desire for more excitement in this lifetime, Lily."

Dejected, Lily nodded mechanically. "Oh."

They climbed the stairs in silence as Lily thought about the rest of her life with a man who preferred to abstain from excitement, audibly sighing her disappointment. As a servant let them in, they found the house empty of the Scott family and William's governess.

"Where is Richard?"

As Lily removed her bonnet, she explained the family had left to visit Elizabeth's family for the day, "Did he mistakenly schedule an appointment with you? He must have forgotten that this day was planned weeks ago."

Mason shook his head. "No. I have no appointment with him."

He found a seat in the parlor as Lily made her way through the room to find a servant. "Would you like some tea?"

Smiling, he said yes and she left to inform the staff. When she returned, Lily sat down beside him.

"Would you like to hear of my time in the war? You seem interested in excitement today, and I think you might enjoy the stories."

Lily plastered a smile on her face as she inwardly hoped Mason wasn't becoming like old Jeremiah Needham, full of war stories but little else. She might be able to withstand an uneventful existence, but one in which he became old Captain Danvers who droned on about boring tales of battles long forgotten? That she was sure she couldn't endure.

But Lily knew polite manners required her to answer yes, so with a smile she answered, "Of course."

For the next hour, Lily heard stories of the desert and the mountains, of battles won and lost, of bravery and treachery. Mason's usually genteel demeanor morphed into one of power and much to her delight, excitement. As she listened, she watched him with growing admiration.

Maybe life wouldn't be so bad with him after all.

Mason finished his story and sat silently for a moment before he said, "What I saw made me understand how much I wanted someone to come home to, Lily."

He lightly touched her fingers, stilling them against her leg. Lily was surprised when her body reacted to his touch, her heart beating faster. She looked down at his hand on hers. Its masculine power covered her small fingers but his touch was gentle.

Would he be like that as a lover? Thoughts of Kadar flashed through her mind, and she abruptly looked up, her wide-eyed gaze meeting Mason's. Snatching her hand away, she quickly stood up.

"I'm sorry, Mason. I'm feeling a bit tired. I hope you understand."

Mason stood and flashed a sympathetic smile. "Of course."

At the door, he leaned down and kissed her hand. "Rest, Lily. It's been an eventful day."

"Yes, I guess it has. Thank you, Mason."

Once he'd left, Lily made her way to her room, truly tired after her time in the country. She lay back on the bed and closed her eyes as fantasies of a life with Kadar danced through her mind as she drifted off to sleep.

Nine

Kadar pressed his lips gently against her nape and whispered, "Today I show you how much I love you, my Lily." He fastened her blindfold and then slowly slid his hands down her neck. She swallowed hard as he pressed his erection into her back, though he knew her reaction was one of arousal, not fear.

"Today I show you how a man truly makes love to a woman."

The gentle heaving of her breasts told of her thoughts even before she spoke. "Please. Yes. Make love to me."

As he had before, he stood in front of her to watch her. "So lovely. I love you in pink. Come to me, Lily."

Lily walked toward him, arms outstretched in front of her. As was the ritual, he let her reach him and rewarded her obedience with a kiss. While he enjoyed her mouth, she pressed her body to his to feel his stiff cock.

Her hands drifted over his stomach, but he grabbed

her wrists before she reached her goal. Looking up at him, she cooed, "Please let me, Kadar."

His erection twitched at her words and although he hadn't planned on this part, he would improvise. "Follow me."

Standing near the couch, he stepped out of his trousers and removed his shirt. Seated, he reclined back to watch her do as he ordered.

"Kneel next to me, Lily."

She stepped toward the couch and tentatively felt around for him. Her hands found his bare thighs, and she lowered herself to the floor.

"Use your hands to explore my body as I have yours," he hoarsely commanded.

Ever compliant, Lily slowly learned about him through her hands. Kadar watched in rapt excitement as her delicate white fingers trailed up his legs to his hips. Her touch was whisper soft, and she seemed to hesitate before moving toward the center of his body.

"Touch me, Lily."

Even more cautiously, she slowly slid her fingers to the V between his legs. Kadar stared in anticipation as she began to tease the nest of brown hair at the base of his cock. Her hands met as they reached the hardness of him, and she wrapped one ladylike hand around him, barely able to hold him.

His cock kicked in her hand, evidence of his desire and delight at what she was doing. She recoiled for a moment, frightened by the movement.

"Don't back away. That's just the effect you have on

me. Don't be afraid."

Lily returned to her position and began gently stroking him, her motions unsure but delightful all the same. Sighing, she moved her hand from the base to the mushroomed cap. "It's so soft, yet hard as steel," she said with almost a tone of wonder in her voice.

Reveling in the touch of her hand on his skin, he moaned and thrust his hips from the couch to encourage her.

"Go faster, Lily."

She obeyed, and he watched as each stroke of her hand moved him closer and closer to that delicious moment of release. But this wasn't what he wanted. When he came, he wanted to be inside her, buried to the hilt, truly joining with her.

Grabbing her hand, he ordered her to stop and undress. Obviously disappointed, she pouted as she did as he directed, and in moments he was looking at her naked body before him.

"Now it's my turn. Lay down on the couch."

Settled between her legs, he maneuvered her into position to get a perfect view of her sex. A dark triangle at the apex of her legs, it glistened with moisture. Licking his lips in anticipation of the taste of her sweetness on his tongue, he began to tease her with his fingers.

"Lily, has anyone ever touched you like this before?"

Shaking her head, she pressed her lips together as he circled her swollen nub.

"Have you ever touched yourself like this?"

To his delight, she nodded. Curious to know more, he

asked, "When? What did you think about?"

He watched as her facial expression changed to show her embarrassment. He wasn't going to let her off that easily, though. Removing his finger, he repeated his question in a far darker tone.

"I can't, Kadar," she whimpered.

Slowly, he dragged his tongue over her inner thigh, stopping just as he reached her cunt. Looking up, he saw her nearly overcome by desire. She'd answer now.

"Tell me."

"At night. When I'm in bed," she said on a sob.

"And?"

Lily hesitated, but the touch of his finger tracing her wet seam convinced her. "You. I think of you."

"That's my Lily. Thank you for telling the truth."

To reward her for her candor, he slid up her body and kissed her sweetly. Propping himself up on his elbow, he lay next to her and let his hand drift over her soft stomach before returning to where it had been.

She spread her legs wider, beckoning him to do more than merely teasing her. God, she was responsive! Everything in his body wanted to plunge into her, but he resisted the urge to rush.

Pressing his mouth to her ear, he began seducing her with words, both scandalous and sweet.

"My Lily, your cunt is so beautiful. Such a delicate pink flower, moist and opened for me. Waiting for my tongue to taste your sweetness."

"Your tongue?"

"My tongue. No man has ever run his tongue over

your cunt making you feel the way you did the last time you were here?"

"No, never," she answered breathlessly.

"Then I will introduce you to a brand new world of pleasure, my love."

Kadar planted soft kisses on her breasts and stomach before positioning himself over her dark curls. Closing his eyes, he inhaled and then licked his lips.

"So beautiful."

With his thumbs, he opened her silky soft folds to see her swollen nub. He gently sucked it, taking it into his mouth and slowly teasing it with his tongue. His cock stiffened rock hard as the first taste of her entered his mouth.

"Kadar..." she began and then her voice trailed off, overcome by passion.

He loved the way her innocence and desire mixed to create a sweet wantonness he hadn't encountered in years. She didn't know not to trust him and her needs wouldn't let her deny him, even if it occurred to her he could hurt her.

Not that he would. He'd long passed the point where he could be careless with her. She was everything to him now.

Slowly, he dragged his tongue over her tender skin, as his thumbs moved to stroke her inner thighs. Her skin quivered under his touch, and with each swipe of his tongue and lips, he inched her closer toward sweet oblivion. He grazed her clit with his teeth ever so gently and heard her whimper his name as she begged for more.

Sensing she was close to the edge, he slid his finger into her. She tugged at his hair and cried out, "Kadar... please...don't stop. Oh my God! I..." as she slid over the edge.

Her body tightened around his finger as she climaxed, her hands clutching his head to her body, as she moaned about wanting more. He lapped up her juices, as desperate as she to please.

When her body ceased its trembling, he returned to her mouth to kiss her and to give her the taste of her body on his tongue.

"Oh Kadar! I never knew a man could make me feel this way. I'm not even ashamed."

Stroking her cheek, he marveled at how she looked even more beautiful than before at that moment. "A woman should never be ashamed of making love. To bring you happiness makes me happy."

"I want to bring you happiness. Tell me what to do."

Kadar's cock moved against her leg as a myriad of thoughts of what he'd like her to do danced through his mind. The more adventurous ones could wait, however. For now, what would make him happiest would be the simplest thing of all: burying himself inside her and making her as happy as she made him.

Sitting up, he took her hand and pulled her to him. "I want you to come with me, Lily."

"Where? I have no clothes on."

"Take my hand and follow me."

Holding his hand tightly, Lily followed him up a secret staircase that led from that room to a bedroom

upstairs. He led her to the bed and sat down, guiding her to sit with him.

"What room is this?"

Kadar began to undo her hair, letting it fall in waves over her shoulders and back. "My bedroom. That couch is fine for foreplay but nothing short of purgatorial for much else."

Turning her face toward him, he kissed her softly. "I've longed for this moment, Lily."

Kadar pulled her onto his lap and she straddled his hips. "I have too. I love you, Kadar."

"Do you trust me?"

"Yes," she said with a smile.

"Even though you've never seen my face?"

"I don't need to see you to know I love you."

"And you know what I want from you?"

"Yes."

"You're willing to submit to me?"

Lily nodded. "Yes, I will do as you say."

Fisting his hand gently in her hair, he tugged slightly. "I won't ask again. If your answer is yes now, it's yes forever."

"Yes, Kadar."

Kissing her deeply, he slid into her. "Ride me, Lily."

The sight of her body taking his into it over and over as her dark waves bounced around her beautiful face almost overwhelmed him. In just a short time, she'd transformed from a shy Victorian woman to a woman who sought to please him sexually in any way possible.

His release inched closer and closer with each slide

into her wet cunt. The feel of her body joining with his, welcoming him into her, was exquisite. He could live forever just as they were now, one with each other. But the reality of their world forced him to question the consequences of their love. Grabbing her by the waist, he stopped her, burying himself as deeply as he could and then stilling both of them.

"Lily, if I stay inside you, I may make you pregnant. I'll ask once: do you wish for me to stop?"

"No! Don't stop!

With her answer, he released his hold on her waist and began to thrust deeply into her as she rode him. When he came, he held her tightly to him and filled her just as she came, her body milking his in complete physical ecstasy.

"Muh tú ra dost darom," he said in a husky voice as she went still in his arms.

"What does that mean?" she asked into the crook of his neck.

"I love you."

He opened his eyes and saw a tear roll down from underneath her blindfold. Wiping it away, he kissed her cheek. "Don't cry."

"I'm sorry. I've just been so lonely since my husband died."

"No more loneliness, my love. You have my undivided attention. I have no one but you."

Kadar eased himself out of her and placed her on the bed. "Stay here. I'll be back in a minute."

When he returned, he stood for a moment to watch her curled up on his bed so innocent and sweet.

She turned toward him and sat up. "Kadar, is something wrong?"

"No. Nothing is wrong."

He sat down next to her and kissed her softly on the cheek. "Do you remember my fantasy?"

Smiling, she nodded. "Is that baklava I smell?"

He placed the plate of pastry next to him and pulled her to him. "Sit between my legs and lean back against me."

Kadar wrapped his arms around her and fed her a piece of baklava, just as he had the first time she'd tasted the dessert. As she ate, he explored her body as if it were his to own.

"I'd like another piece, please," she said sweetly, her face turned toward his.

"Of course. Anything for my Lily. And you'll need your strength in a few minutes, so enjoy."

After licking his fingers, she asked, "Need my strength?"

"Yes. We're not finished."

He heard a small moan escape her lips. "You like that?"

"Yes," she crooned. "I like the idea of you making love to me again."

"Good."

Nuzzling her neck, he kissed her behind the ear as his hand made its way to the dark triangle between her legs. He stroked her softly and loved how her legs fell open to provide him better access.

"I love this...its softness and pinkness. The way you

moan when I rub your clit."

Lily placed her hand over his to show her agreement. "I love the way you talk about my body as if it brings you joy."

"It does. Every part of you brings me joy, my love."

Kadar continued to stroke her until he was sure she was ready. "I want you on your hands and knees."

He knew she had no experience with this sexual position, but her willingness to obey his wishes pleased him. When she'd done as he'd said, he sat up behind her, gently placed his hands on her hips, and leaned forward to kiss her.

"Lily, don't be afraid. This is just another way for me to make love to you."

"I'm not afraid. I love all the ways you make love to me."

Slowly, he entered her from behind, careful not to plunge in too fast and frighten her. Reaching around her, he returned to stroking her slick folds above where they were joined.

Lily tentatively pushed back against his body, his cue that she was ready. He held on to her hips and began to move in and out of her with more passion. He pumped in and out, his flesh slapping off hers.

Her moans filled the room, exciting him more. "Take all of me, Lily."

"Yes," she said in a whimper.

Kadar backed off from her body to allow himself room to slide a finger between her cheeks. With his fingertip, he massaged her virgin hole and felt her body respond,

tightening around his cock.

She was close. Just a little more...

With a gentle nudge of his finger, he breeched her virgin passage and pushed in slowly.

"Kadar! I can't hold on!"

"Come for me, Lily. Come now."

In the next moment, her body was milking his cock and squeezing against his finger, softly grasping and releasing. It wasn't long before his own orgasm exploded into her, flooding her with his hot liquid.

Kadar held her tightly to him, their bodies pressed against one another as each one took and received from the other. Never before had he felt so completely joined with another.

As he lay with Lily in his arms, her head on his chest, he marveled at how much he adored her. Never in his life had he wanted — no, needed — a woman like he did her.

She'd submitted her heart and trust to him. Everything he'd ever wanted in a woman she offered him. Now he wanted more, though.

Now he wanted her solely as his forever.

Gently, he nudged her awake. "Lily, it's time to go home."

"I don't want to leave, Kadar."

"The afternoon must end. But you'll come back to me tomorrow."

Kissing his chest, she looked up at him and innocently asked, "Will there ever be a time when I may stay?"

The reality of her life provided them the answer to that question.

"You're a young widow. Has your brother chosen a potential suitor to be your new husband?"

Lily laid silently, her head above his heart.

"Your silence tells me the answer. But we'll enjoy one another until then."

Lily sat up and faced him, her blindfold still fastened on her head. "Is that all this is? Enjoying me? I love you. You're all I can think about. When you make love to me, I feel like you care about me. Don't you?"

God, how much he wished he could see her eyes, even though he was sure they were filled with pain at that moment. He caressed her cheek and cupped it as she leaned into his hand.

"More than you know, my Lily. No other woman can claim my heart like you can. I think of little else but you. You've enchanted me, and when I make love to you, I feel like I've finally found home. You are everything I've ever desired in a woman."

"Then ask my brother for the right to take me as your wife!" she cried. "Don't let another man take me away!"

Lily slouched, her shoulders rounded in sadness. Kadar pulled her to him and held her close. Rubbing her back, he whispered, "Don't be upset. Everything will end up for the best. I promise."

Ten

Lily dressed for her date with Mason but couldn't stop herself from reminiscing about her time with Kadar almost twenty-four hours earlier. The sensations his touch created in her! For the first time, she thought of herself as desirable, and she loved the feeling.

Fixing her hair in the mirror, she stopped as she caught a glimpse of herself. Something in the way her green eyes looked back at her showed a change in her. No longer did she present the appearance of the proper Englishwoman she always had. Something in her face told of her experiences with Kadar.

Running her fingertips over her cheek as he had, she studied the newly sensual face staring back at her and wondered if anyone else saw the change that had begun in her.

Noises from downstairs told her Mason had arrived. Lily took a deep breath and left the safety of her room to begin their date. Mason waited for her at the bottom of the steps and watched her move toward him, his eyes fixed on her as if there were no one else on earth at that moment but her.

"Lily, you look beautiful," he said as he took her hand in his. "I thought we'd take a walk through the park today. Would you like that?"

Smiling, she nodded, but in truth her heart wished she was in Hertfordshire in the arms of the man she loved and feared she would soon have to give up.

"That would be very nice. It's a lovely day for a stroll around the park."

Lily walked beside Mason as they wound their way through Regent's Park and the dozens of other local citizens there to enjoy the spring weather. The colors of the season showed in the pink cherry blossoms that hung from the trees and the purples, reds, and yellows of the flowers that lined the walkway. In the green, children played and an artist painted at an easel.

He could be painting her future. A perfectly respectable future. She'd move from her brother's home in Regent's Park to Mason's. She'd become the lady of his home—Mrs. Mason Danvers—and the mother to his children, who a nanny would push in a carriage along the very pathway she walked now as she stayed at home and planned dinner parties and other affairs people of their station attended.

Until recently, this would have been enough for her. But everything had changed.

Mason's voice roused her out of her daydreaming. "Lily, let's sit at the pavilion and talk."

He guided her by the arm to a bench inside the pavilion and sat beside her, his face the look of anticipation. She knew what was on his mind and prepared herself to accept his proposal.

"I'm sure you know how I feel about you, Lily. I've made no secret of my affection for you."

"I do know, Mason."

"Then you surely know what I'm about to ask. I know I'm not the kind of man you may find appealing at first glance. I'm a military man, trained to fight, but I swear I'm no brute and promise to take care of you for all our days together."

Brute.

Mason's choice of words made her moments with Kadar flood her mind. *Force is for brutes.*

Was it right to agree to be Mason's wife when she loved another? As Lily listened to him give his well-rehearsed proposal, guilt gnawed at her conscience. Mason may be exactly what he said he was. He may even be that brash man she'd believed he was when they'd first met. Whatever he was, did he deserve to marry a woman whose heart belonged to another?

"Will you marry me, Lily?"

Mason's deep brown eyes searched her face as he tried to interpret the silence that met his proposal. Looking into them, she found it impossible to tell him she loved another man, a man who had awakened feelings in her that would have to be forgotten if she became Mrs.

Mason Danvers.

Sadness tugged at her heart. Kadar would have to be forgotten also if she agreed to be Mason's wife. How could she forget the one soul who had touched her deeper than any other in this world?

But life gave her no choice.

"Are you sure you want me, Mason? I can be quite stubborn and willful."

A sly smile spread across Mason's lips and a sparkle she'd never seen before appeared in his eyes. "Stubborn and willful? I've never witnessed that in you."

"Well, I can be. You should know that before I agree to marry you."

Mason bent down to kiss the top of her hand and seductively looked up at her. "I'm sure you're exaggerating. Something tells me you are far less willful than you claim."

Lily felt her face warm in a blush at the reality she'd discovered with Kadar. No, she wasn't stubborn or willful but, in fact, craved the permission to be exactly the opposite.

"There's no need to be embarrassed, Lily. I love you just the way you are."

"Then I say yes, Mason. I will marry you."

Lily's guilt grew with each person who congratulated them on their engagement. Mason beamed with each retelling of how lucky he was to be marrying such a fine lady, while she secretly planned on meeting Kadar one last time. When Mason announced to her that he had an

appointment he must attend to, a sense of relief came over her. She'd be free to go to Kadar.

All the way to Hertfordshire, she wrestled with her feelings for Mason and Kadar. As much as she wished she could marry Kadar, the reality of her life dictated that she marry the captain, a respectable man accepted by society.

In some way, she did care for Mason, but those feelings were dwarfed by what she felt for Kadar. She'd marry Mason knowing that the only man who'd ever made her truly feel sensual and beautiful wasn't her husband but someone whose face she'd never seen.

In his study, Kadar eagerly waited for that day's meeting with Lily. Their last time together the day before had proven to him that she was ready. Not only did she desire him, but she trusted him. Now she was ready to explore his world.

"Will you require anything this afternoon, Master?"

Kadar's daydreams about what that day's rendezvous promised receded at the sound of his servant's voice. "Yes, Akil. Bring me the cat o'nine tails."

"Will that be all?"

"And make sure to brew tea and have it in my bedroom."

"Yes, Master. Should I show the lady to that room instead today?"

"Yes."

Moments later, Akil returned with the cat o'nine tails.

Taking it from him, Kadar excused him and returned to planning for Lily's arrival. Today they would explore their relationship in ways he knew she'd never even thought of, let alone experienced. Today's events would be a drastic test of her trust in him. Would she still trust him afterward?

The soft leather of the whip he dragged across his palm excited him. His favorite sexual toy, it delivered the perfect mixture of pain and pleasure in his hands. Just the thought of its sharp caress touching Lily's soft skin made his cock stiffen.

He heard her carriage rumble to a stop in front of the house and stood to watch as she walked to the door. These few moments in which he could see her eyes thrilled him each time she visited. The blindfold was a useful prop, but he longed for a day when he'd gaze into those expressive green eyes that at that very moment seemed so full of emotion.

From the doorway of his study, he spied Akil escort her to the second floor. Through the secret staircase, he made his way to the bedroom. There he watched her carefully place the now commonplace blindfold over her eyes and tie the silk strings behind her head. He hadn't instructed Akil to tell her where to stand, so she stood next to the bed, her hands on a bedpost for security.

Padding up behind her, Kadar spoke in his usual whispered tone. "How is my Lily today?"

"I missed you so," she answered sadly.

Her voice touched him, and he wrapped his arms around her shoulders. "Why so sad?"

Twisting in his hold, she turned toward him and buried her face in his chest. "Please don't make me talk about it. I don't want to cry."

Kadar gently rubbed her back to soothe her. "There. Nothing can be so bad if we're together."

"Oh, Kadar!" she cried as tears began to roll over her cheeks from under the blindfold.

Brushing away her tears, he said, "Shhh. No more crying. Tell me what's wrong."

"Please, no. All I want is you to make love to me so I can forget everything but the time I get to spend with you—my life, the expectations of everyone, what I'm supposed to want. I want to get lost in the world we create here."

He cradled her face in his hands and kissed her, desperately wanting to replace her sorrow with happiness. She responded as she never had before.

"Make me forget, Kadar."

The sharp sound of need in her words made him want her more than ever. Quickly, he removed her dress and undergarments as she tore at his shirt and pants to reach his bare skin. He fed off her sadness and took it from her as he worshipped her body with his mouth. As she moaned her pleasure, he trailed kisses over her skin, licking and nipping her breasts and stomach, all in the hopes of making the world that had upset her fade from existence, even if only for a short time.

"I love you, Kadar. Please tell me you love me. Tell me this isn't all a dream I'll forget when I'm forced to wake. I don't want to forget this."

He released her nipple from his mouth and returned to kiss her. "Muh tú ra dost darom, my beautiful Lily," he whispered against her lips.

"Take me, Kadar. Show me your love and let me show you mine."

Scooping her up in his arms, he placed her on the bed and covered her with his body. Needing her as much as she needed him, he fought to restrain his desire, but it was too great. He plunged into her, searching for that sweet moment of release they could provide one another.

Her nails raked over his back as he thrust into her, and her moans pushed him on to give her that moment that would allow her to forget the world. Her body met each invasion eagerly, welcoming him over and over into her.

"Kadar...oh, Kadar," she groaned in a voice that sounded desperate and sad.

"Forget the world. There's only the two of us. Let me take your sadness, Lily."

Like one wanting to push away what threatened the one he loved, he worked to force out all the things that had upset her, as if the act of making love could eliminate her unhappiness. At some point—he didn't know when—the physical act transcended every experience he'd ever had with women, and he was sure he couldn't stand to be away from her for another day.

When he came, he took her body with him over that delicious edge and for a few, brief moments, he knew he'd succeeded in making her forget everything but him.

They lay silently for a long time, still joined as one

comprised of two separate beings who longed for nothing more than to be with one another.

"You've changed me. I saw it in the mirror today," she said quietly near his ear.

Softly stroking her back, he said, "Changed you? No. You are as you've always been."

"I'm different now, and it's because of you. You've brought out something in me, Kadar. I crave the feel of your touch. I dream of the things you do to me, and I want more."

"You've always wanted those things, Lily. If you didn't, you wouldn't have come back to me after the first time you came here."

Lily buried her face in his neck. "Who am I? What am I becoming?"

"The sensual and desirable woman you were meant to be. The woman who threatens to undo the control of this man."

Lily crawled on top of him and moved to fit her body onto his. Wiggling her behind, she asked sweetly, "Control?"

Kadar knew what she meant and slapped his palm against her bottom. "Control."

"No one's ever done that to me before. I had no idea I liked it."

Squeezing both cheeks in his hands, he moved her cunt over his swelling cock. She was wet and open for him, but he wanted something else before he returned to that.

"Lily, I want to try something new with you. I promise

you'll like it as much as when I spank you."

"Okay. What?"

"I want you to stand on the floor and hold on to the bedpost."

Kadar saw a slight trepidation in her movements and hugged her from behind as she stood by the corner of the bed. "Trust me."

He grabbed the cat o'nine tails from a nearby table and ran the whips through his fingers. Standing behind her, he lightly dragged the leather toy over her hip.

"Do you know what this is?"

Lily stood silently for a few moments, as if she were trying to figure out what she'd felt move across her skin. Shaking her head, she said quietly, "No."

Wrapping his arms around her waist, he dragged it over her stomach while he kissed a trail up and down her neck. "It's called a cat o'nine tails, Lily. And when I use this on your soft skin, the sensation will be exquisite. Tell me you want me to use this on you, my Lily."

Breathlessly, she answered, "Yes," as she pressed her back into his body. "But please let me take off the blindfold. Please let me see you."

He knew he should deny her request, but he so much wanted to see her eyes wide with passion after that first moment when the leather hit her skin. Placing the handle of his toy in his mouth, he untied the ribbons of the blindfold and slipped it off her head.

As he waited for her eyes to adjust, he readied himself behind her, cat o'nine tails in hand, ready to introduce her to another part of his world.

Eleven

Slowly, Lily's eyes adjusted to the light and she saw the deep reds and browns of Kadar's room. The bed where they'd just made love stood in front of her, its dark crimson sheets wrinkled and disheveled from their passion.

The man she'd waited to see stood behind her with something he promised would delight her. She'd smelled the leather of it a minute earlier and a tiny fear had spiked in her brain.

But she trusted him.

"Hang on to the bedpost, Lily."

As always, she'd obey him, but she wanted to see his face before they began. She needed to see the man she loved. Like a child eager to see a surprise, she spun around to see his face for the first time and was dumbstruck.

"No! No! It can't be!" she wailed.

She saw him begin to explain, but all she heard was

the word "No!" screaming in her brain.

"How could you do this? You lied to me! You called yourself Kadar. Your name isn't Kadar! Your name is Mason!"

Slowly, he put the cat o'nine tails down on the bed and moved toward her. "I didn't lie, Lily. I'm also called Kadar by those I knew in Afghanistan."

"You tricked me! And don't talk like him! No more whispering. Use your own voice."

"I didn't. You came to me wanting what I had to offer."

Kadar touched her arm lightly, but she quickly backed away. Confusion grew in her as the look on his face signaled his hurt. How could he be hurt? She was the one who'd been deceived!

"But you knew who I was and intentionally kept your identity a secret. I'm such a fool! What an idiot I am! Letting a total stranger blindfold me and do the things you did."

Suddenly she remembered she was stark naked and rushed to regain her modesty by covering herself with her hands.

"I admit I knew who you were, even though I hadn't begun courting you. I wanted you as much as you wanted me."

Lily frantically struggled to get into her dress. At least being clothed might lessen the humiliation, she hoped.

"I didn't want you! I wanted Kadar!" she cried. "You're just the man my brother believes can take me off his hands. But Kadar was different."

All at once the emotion of the situation came over her and she began to cry, covering her face as she sobbed.

"Lily, don't cry. I am Kadar. Even though you know me as Mason, the man you know me as here loves you. Please sit down with me."

"No, I will not! And I won't marry you! How could I knowing who you really are?"

"You won't marry me because of my sexual preferences—preferences you just told me you want more of?"

"That's not what I meant and you know it!"

He was twisting her words and she wasn't going to let him get away with it. And then the entire truth occurred to her.

"Oh my God! Just how many pupils have you had?"

Smirking, he answered, "I don't understand. It was fine when I was Kadar that I'd been with other women, but now as Mason, it's not fine?"

Wiping her tearstained face, she screamed, "It wasn't fine for Kadar either!"

Gently, he touched her arm again. "Lily, I know it was wrong to deceive you, but I love you. Can you forgive me? I'm still Kadar in many ways."

Lily wasn't sure if she was angry, hurt, or disappointed or a mixture of all three, but she was sure she couldn't forgive him. Roughly, she yanked her arm away from his fingers and wrapped her arms around her body hoping to find some comfort.

"You lied to me. You let me fall in love with you, but it was all a lie."

Mason sat down on the bed and stared up at her, his eyes full of sadness. Nothing he could say would fix what he'd done, but Lily stood still, hoping he'd say that one magic thing that would make everything between them better.

Quietly, he said, "I'll apologize for everything, but not for what I feel or wanting you to love me in return."

She wanted to forgive him, to have him take her in his arms and hold her. But she couldn't.

Lowering her head, she looked into the face of the man she'd imagined a thousand times. "Goodbye, Mason."

He watched her walk away knowing he could do nothing to change her mind. He'd gambled and lost. Disgusted with himself, he wondered how he could have even believed she'd accept his behavior. What a fool he'd been!

Mason slowly dressed and returned to his study, feeling that already the house seemed emptier without her in it. Sitting slouched in his chair, his body clearly telegraphing his emotions, he tried to convince himself that this time was no different than when any other woman had ceased to be in his life, but it was no use.

Lily wasn't just any other woman.

A knock at the door made his heart leap in expectation, but when he opened it, he only saw Akil.

"What do you need?"

"Nothing, Master. I simply wanted to ensure there was nothing you needed."

Mason turned away from the door and sat once again

in his chair as the servant followed. After some time had passed, he noticed Akil still standing in front of him.

"Is there something you need, Akil?"

"No, Master. I haven't been excused and you haven't given me any orders."

"I don't have any to give."

"Master?"

Mason looked up at the man's confused expression but felt no interest in acting like the master of anything at the moment.

"We'll be returning to the city in a short while."

"Yes, Master."

Akil remained standing as still as a statue before Mason. When he met the servant's gaze, he knew he was waiting to comment on the events of the afternoon.

"Akil, you obviously require something, so speak up."

"Master, I noticed Mrs. Norville left in haste today."

Mason bristled at his servant's use of Lily's formal name. "Be careful, Akil. While you may be far more than a typical servant, you're treading on dangerous ground."

Bowing, the servant quickly scrambled to show his respect. "Please forgive me, Master Kadar. I meant no offense."

Mason blew the air out of his lungs in frustration. "I know, I know. You've been a loyal member of my household for long enough for me to be sure you meant no harm."

"Thank you."

"But I sense that you feel you need to tell me

something."

"Master, please forgive me, but you've forgotten who you are. You were given the name Kadar by my people because you were powerful enough to rescue my village. They may call you Mason in this land, but that doesn't change who you are."

Mason considered his servant's words and remembered the event that gave him his name. Caught in the middle between their country's forces and British forces, Akil's family and neighbors had been helpless to protect themselves against both sides' attacks. A little cunning had enabled him to rescue Akil, Nuha, and thirty others before the Afghan forces had overrun their town. His commanding officer had acceded to his requests to help everyone to safety, and Mason had made it his responsibility to watch over the two people who now worked as his servants.

Mason ran his fingers through his hair and closed his eyes. He wore the name Akil and his people had given him with pride, but in England, Kadar had been reduced to showing his power in the tawdry underground world of Victorian sexuality.

"Not all exhibitions of power are equal, Akil."

"Very true, Master, but one who has shown the power to do as you did for my people can surely persuade one woman to return to him."

"It's not power that's needed here."

Akil bowed deeply. "As you say, Master."

Alone, Mason weighed his options concerning Lily. Every choice led back to one ending: he didn't want a

life without her. And if that meant changing the way he thought about power, then so be it.

By the time she arrived home, Lily had cried enough to last a lifetime. Only when she'd lost Jeremy had she cried more. This was different, though. Losing a husband should affect a woman, but what she felt in her heart at losing Kadar seemed wrong to her.

Unless she truly loved him.

The truth of what she felt for him nagged at her with each denial she fabricated. She couldn't be in love with him.

But she was.

She shouldn't feel this emptiness from the loss of him.

But she did.

Lily dried her eyes as the carriage slowed to a stop in front of Richard's Frederick Street home. One deep breath and she readied herself for the outside world. She may be in love with Kadar—Mason—and she may even feel lost now because what they had was over, but she had to be strong because she'd meant what she'd said back in Hertfordshire.

She would not marry Mason.

"Aunty Lily!"

As she stepped out of the carriage, Lily looked up to see William and his governess on their way out of the house. She didn't dread seeing him anymore, but on this occasion found herself truly happy to see her nephew coming toward her.

"Come with us to the park, Aunty Lily. Please?" the boy whined.

Lily looked at the governess, who seemed to instinctively understand now was not the time for a stroll in the park.

"William, your aunt has just returned from her day out and could use some rest. Let's leave her be."

Lily smiled at the younger woman, not even caring that she probably knew more than she should.

"But I never see you anymore," William complained.

In truth, her nephew was right. Lately, if she wasn't traveling to Hertfordshire, she was spending time with Mason. The realization that, in fact, both activities had involved the same person struck her as she stood on the sidewalk and for a moment she became lost in her sadness.

"Pleeease!"

William's wheedling shook her from her thoughts. Lily mussed her nephew's hair and smiled. "I promise tomorrow we can enjoy the park together."

The boy's lips curled into a pout for a second, but just as quickly he returned to the well-mannered child he'd become and smiled up at her. As his governess expertly guided him toward the fun that awaited him at the park, he turned back and yelled, "I can't wait for tomorrow, Aunty Lily!" before he began running down the street.

Climbing the stairs to the front door, Lily reflected on the tremendous change in her nephew. In such a short time, he'd transformed from an insolent terror no one

could tolerate to a loving child she welcomed spending time with.

William wasn't the only member of the house who'd changed. Whether she wanted to accept it or not, she knew in just as brief a time she'd changed from the average Englishwoman she'd always considered herself to be to a woman who felt sensual and beautiful. She knew she had only one person to thank for her awakening.

Kadar.

Mason.

That was the problem, wasn't it? As Kadar, he was the one she thanked for introducing her to a world of sensual delights like she'd never dreamed of before. However, as Mason, he was the person she blamed for deceiving her and dashing her fantasies to pieces. That they were the same person confused and troubled her, throwing her emotions into turmoil.

"Lily, did you see William and Miss Allen? I think they were planning to invite you to join them on their trip to the park."

"I did, Elizabeth," Lily said quietly.

Lily's voice was shaky and she instantly saw the concern on her sister-in-law's face.

"Is everything all right? Did something upset you while you were out shopping?"

The lie she told each time she left to rendezvous with Kadar hung in the air, and she quickly answered, "It's fine. I just feel tired this afternoon. Please excuse me, Elizabeth. I think I'll just go to my room to lie down."

With Elizabeth's blessing, Lily climbed the stairs to

her room and sunk into the bed, exhausted from the day's events.

"Lily, dear. Mason's downstairs. Are you feeling any better?"

Slowly, Lily opened her eyes to see Elizabeth leaning over her, concern written all over her face.

"I'm sorry. Can you please tell Mason I won't be able to see him?"

Elizabeth stroked her hair and pressed her palm to her cheek. "Of course, dear. Can I get you a sleeping draught?"

"That would be wonderful. Thank you."

As Lily listened to Elizabeth rejoin Richard and Mason downstairs, she tried to block out their conversation, but it was impossible.

"Is she ill?" Mason asked, his tone full of worry.

"She is sorry, but she says she can't see you, Mason."

Lily cringed at Elizabeth's characterization of her as sorry. She wasn't sorry, at least not about avoiding him. That her sister-in-law had told him she couldn't see him exactly as she'd said it without the addition of the word "tonight" made her feel a little better, though. She didn't want to see him that night, tomorrow, and if she could help it, ever again.

"Please tell her I send her my best wishes for a rapid recovery."

Lily lay in bed wondering why Mason said things like that. "Kadar would never speak like that," she mumbled as she rolled over to escape the conversation.

As soon as she'd said the words, she silently corrected herself. *Stop that! Mason is Kadar, and Kadar is Mason. You can't keep thinking they're different people.*

Twelve

Lily was relieved to find that she could remain in bed for the better part of the next two days. Richard, like most men, assumed she was suffering from some female malady and never questioned her absence. Elizabeth may have sensed that she was feigning sickness, but to Lily's relief, she said nothing about it. Best of all, Mason didn't return.

Sitting at the breakfast table, she sipped her morning tea and absentmindedly flipped through the newspaper. The warmer weather had settled into Regent's Park, and bees buzzed around the honeysuckle bush below the open window. Inhaling the flowers' sweet fragrance, Lily closed her eyes and concentrated on the beautiful day that lay ahead of her.

"Are you feeling better today, sister?"

Opening her eyes, she saw Richard settling in to his chair to begin breakfast.

"A little."

"Mason was concerned about you. I spoke to him yesterday afternoon, and he asked about you."

"That's nice of him," she murmured as she returned her attention to the newspaper.

"I'm very pleased you two have gotten on so well, Lily. I know you were hesitant at first, but I think you can agree he's a fine man. You'll have a good life together."

Lily forced a weak smile and nodded. There was no point in trying to change Richard's mind this morning. She just wasn't up to it.

While her brother ate, she focused on the Times, hoping her brother would depart to begin his workday and leave her in peace. Her wish was granted just a short time later, but as she skimmed the Agony Column, she was greeted by yet another reminder that she wasn't truly free of Mason quite yet.

"M. misses L. and urgently wishes to reunite with her."

Lily closed the newspaper and sat back in disgust. Mason had posted a notice similar to that one the day before, which had made her nothing but irritated.

"Does he think I need to be reminded every day of his feelings?" she wondered aloud.

For Lily, the idea that Mason would use the Agony Column to relay messages to her — the very place she'd found Kadar — was too much. She'd kept alive the tiniest hope that she'd find a notice from Kadar one of these mornings that would tell her his longing for her was like hers for him. Instead, what she read were the words

Mason would use, at once flowery and almost officious.

But she knew the truth that Mason was part of Kadar and vice versa. She still loved the man, regardless of what she called him. That's why his deceit hurt so much.

Rising from the table, she pushed the paper away from her. She couldn't go on thinking about him, even if her brother wanted her to marry him. Today was the start of a new life for her.

"William, please eat your oatmeal."

Lily looked up from her breakfast to wait for her nephew's reaction. For so long he'd been so difficult, it was a habit to cringe at any request made of him.

"Yes, Mother."

Everyone around the table let out a collective sigh of relief, and Lily winked at him to show how impressed she was at his behavior. As she looked at the relaxed look on Elizabeth's face, Lily smiled at her happiness and congratulated herself for being the architect of William's change. The governess she'd chosen had worked miracles, and the child's transformation had changed everyone around him.

As the rest of the family scattered to begin their day, Lily took the time to consider an idea that had nagged at her since she'd seen Mason's second Agony Column message. Could she truly condemn him for acting one way in public and another in private?

Yes, he'd deceived her, but as both Mason and Kadar, he'd never shown her anything but sweetness and love. And hadn't she intentionally meant to deceive him as she

allowed Mason to court her while secretly sneaking off to meet Kadar in the countryside? That she never truly did deceive him didn't alter the fact that she'd believed she was and had been fine with her own actions.

The truth of the matter was that both had hidden their behavior in Hertfordshire, but it was that time with Kadar that she missed most. Each visit to his home had aroused something deep inside her she didn't want to lose.

For the third day in a row, she read the Times Agony Column hoping today would be the day she saw a message from Kadar. In her heart, she knew she would eventually relent and see Mason again. More than because she had to was because she wanted to. She loved him and could forgive him. But it was Kadar she truly missed.

Like each time before, she read the notices detailing the misery and loss of her fellow Londoners, feeling each writer's suffering with every word. Her heart went out to a woman seeking her long lost love she'd missed for decades and the man desperate to regain the love of a woman who'd left him for another.

And then she saw it.

"K. will see L. at his home in Regent's park at three today."

Excitement raced through her body as she savored the sound of each word as she read his message aloud again and again. It was a command, but its gentleness touched her, arousing her even as she sat alone in the breakfast room.

She would go to him as he ordered. She had no

choice. He was the man she adored, and he'd realized what made her happy. To have the private Kadar, she'd marry the public Mason.

Mason's Regent's Park home was smaller and far less secluded than his Hertfordshire home, but he needed to show Lily that Kadar was a part of him even in their proper London suburb. He'd tried to win her back as Mason and had failed. She didn't want to return to the man who wore the face of a proper English gentleman because society dictated it. She wanted the man who'd introduced her to a different world, a world he knew she craved.

So he'd give her that man.

At three o'clock she arrived, and as he'd instructed Akil to do, he showed her into the study. Kadar waited in an alcove and watched with a full heart as she positioned herself with her back toward the window, just as she'd always done in Hertfordshire.

His heart leaped in joy as he saw her acceptance of him. Quietly, he moved behind her as he always had, and wrapped his hands around her neck. He leaned in next to her ear and kissed her sweetly.

"My Lily. Tell me why you returned to me," he whispered.

She leaned back to feel his body against hers and swallowed hard. "I missed my Kadar."

The need in her voice sent a jolt through his body, and instantly his cock was hard. He'd missed her too.

This time would be different, though.

Slowly, he turned her to face him and looked into those gorgeous green eyes he'd waited so long to see as Kadar. He tipped her head up toward his and bent down to kiss her deeply, loving the feel of her soft lips on his. Drawing her to him, he buried his hand in her hair to release it from its pins. It tumbled over her shoulders, covering his hands, and he pulled back to look at her.

"That's how I love to see my Lily."

Shyly, she smiled up at him. "I love you. I know you must be Mason Danvers to the rest of the world, but can you always be Kadar with me?"

He was sure his heart filled more than it ever had at her request. No more would he be forced to indulge his fantasies with frustrated society women. Finally, he'd found a woman who truly accepted his desires and wanted to share them with him.

"Always."

Lily's wrapped her arms around him and nuzzled his neck. "Please make love to me. I need to feel you again."

Quickly, he drew the curtains and stripped her clothes from her as she worked to unbutton his shirt and trousers. In seconds, he lifted her to him, positioning his cock at her wet entrance and teasing her with the tip.

Kissing him desperately, she wriggled in his arms to force him to bury himself inside her. "Please, Kadar. Don't make me wait!"

Turning to his right, he placed her on the edge of his desk and carefully lowered her to her back. She impatiently wrapped her legs around his waist and pulled him toward her.

"Hurry, please. I need you inside me."

Looking down into those beautiful eyes pleading for him to satisfy her, he couldn't deny her and let his self-control slip away as he buried his cock in her slick channel. Her body welcomed him home with every thrust, and he reveled in the joy of making love to the woman he'd spend the rest of his life with. Bending over, he took her in his arms as they came together, each giving the other the acceptance they sought.

Kadar carried her to the couch and placed her between his legs as he leaned back against the arm. Pressing her body to his, she whispered, "Your fantasy."

"Exactly. And it can't be my fantasy without your favorite treat."

From a table behind the couch, he took a piece of baklava from a plate and placed it in her mouth.

"I love this fantasy, Kadar. It's so delicious to have you hold me as you feed me."

"I'm happy you love it. I want nothing more than your happiness."

Lily moaned her pleasure as he fed her another piece of the dessert. "Kadar, please promise me it will always be like this."

Kadar ran his hands over her breasts, tenderly teasing her nipples, and then to her stomach, stopping just above the juncture of her legs. Every inch of her excited him, and he wanted to spend the rest of his time on Earth exploring every part of her to take her body to heights she'd never thought possible.

"Your submission is a gift I cherish, Lily. I promise to always adore you as I do right now."

He slid one long finger into the dark triangle and teased her swollen clit before plunging into her. With his other hand he gently encircled her neck. One finger led to two, and she writhed in ecstasy under his control.

She was so wet, so open to him. Each dip into her cunt covered his fingers in her juices, and his stiff cock pressed against his belly, wanting what his fingers were enjoying. A few swift movements and she'd be on top of him, his cock buried to the balls in her.

But he wanted something else.

"Let's continue where we left off," he whispered as his fingers trailed over her inner thigh.

"Where we left off?"

Kadar heard the uncertainty in her voice but dismissed it. He wouldn't be much of a Dominant if he couldn't calm his woman.

Guiding her up from the couch, he stood her on her feet. "Stand here."

He slipped into his pants and reached into the desk drawer for the cat o'nine tails. As he did, he saw Lily reach for her dress.

"No. You stay undressed."

Coming out from behind the desk, Kadar saw her eyes grow wide.

"Kadar?"

He heard the fear in her voice but was sure there was curiosity and possibly desire buried underneath. "This will make you feel as wonderful as when I spanked you with my hand, my love. Now hold on to the arm of the couch."

Lily did just as she was ordered and Kadar positioned himself behind her. His eyes traveled over her porcelain white skin as he tenderly stroked her back and hips, slipping his hand over her bottom. Gently, he prepared her for the mixture of pain and pleasure he would soon deliver. Caressing her back and legs, he explained the ways of his world.

"Lily, I'm a Dominant and you're my submissive. That doesn't mean I would ever hurt you or your emotional and physical safety aren't important to me, but it does mean how we make love is different than how you and your husband did."

He stopped talking to kiss her softly on the lips and then continued. "If you ever become frightened, I want you to say the word "sweet" and I'll change what I'm doing. And if you ever need me to stop, I want you to say the word "apple." Do you understand?"

In a tiny voice, she answered, "Yes."

"I would never hurt you, Lily. I told you when we met that force is for brutes and blackguards."

Turning her head to see him, she met his gaze and he saw nothing but love in her eyes. "I trust you, Kadar. I willingly submit to you."

After softly placing a kiss in the middle of her back, he took one last look at her pale skin and flicked his wrist to bring the cat o'nine tails to her back. The buttery leather whips left their mark and instantly her skin began to pinken.

Lily's obvious shock was evident in her sharp intake of breath, but she quickly calmed and just as he had when he'd spanked her, he tenderly smoothed her heated skin with his hand.

"My Lily," he whispered as he readied the toy again.

Once more, he swung the whips toward her back, delivering the sting each inflicted. Lily's hands gripped the arm of the couch tightly, her knuckles whitening, but Kadar knew one or two more swipes would change her fear to desire.

He soothed the skin with his palm, stroking her pain into comfort as he sensed her relax at his touch. "One more, love."

One more became two and then three and as he'd believed, by the last time the leather touched her skin, she was almost consumed by need. Lovingly, he caressed her skin to sweet relief as she begged to touch him.

"Please, I need to kiss you, to feel you. Please, Kadar!"

"Turn around."

He forgave her for not knowing a submissive's proper role and let her take the lead for a moment when she pressed her mouth to his, so desperate to connect with him in her arousal. Her hands slid over his chest and shoulders as her lips and tongue took from his every ounce of pleasure he could offer.

"Tell me what my Lily wants."

"Satisfy my need, Kadar."

In a moment, he was out of his pants and on top of her on the couch, his body melding with hers into one. He entered her in one sharp thrust, their bodies joining in perfect pleasure. Her body clung to his, her cunt sweetly welcoming his cock each time as he sought that spot in her that would make her shatter into a million pieces. Her mouth devoured his, and she moaned her pleasure into him, exciting him more. More than ever before, he needed to satisfy her need to satisfy his own. When she finally cried out to signal her orgasm, he held her close to him as her shaking body dragged his own release from him. They lay for a long time in each other's arms, their heartbeats and breathing the only sounds in the room.

For Kadar, this was everything he'd dreamed of since he'd returned home. There was just one more thing to do.

In her ear, he said, "Time to go, Lily."

The look on her face as she sat upright was full of hurt and confusion. "Why?"

Kadar smiled. "It's time we found the vicar. We've got a honeymoon to begin. How does a week in Hertfordshire sound?"

Lily kissed him and rested her head on his chest. "Perfect. Will there be baklava?"

The End

Look for *Masquerade*,
another Gabrielle Bisset novella
set in Victorian England!

EXCERPT

"**A**re you enjoying yourself, Count? You don't dance?"

"Not particularly well, my lady, but I will make an exception for you."

Behind her mask, Annelisa beamed. This was going to be even easier than she'd hoped. "Perhaps later. For now, I prefer to enjoy your company this way."

She watched as relief washed over him and his body relaxed.

"I think I'd like to take a walk outside for some fresh air. Would you care to join me, sir?"

"Absolutely."

Taking her arm in his, he guided her through the library to the outside. As they strolled around the well-manicured Italian gardens famous to the Stewart mansion, they made thoughtful conversation while Annelisa's eyes scanned the area for the place she'd bring her plan to fruition.

Just the way he spoke to her as if she were an intelligent being impressed her. She'd made a good choice in Nikolai, but as they continued to walk the mansion's grounds, she worried he might be a little too respectful to do what she needed him to do.

Subtly, she began stroking his arm with her free hand and then slid her gloved fingers inside his sleeve to touch his wrist. Even through the fabric, she felt the heat of his skin and sensed his pulse begin to quicken as they continued their conversation.

She was sure he was interested. Now if she could induce him to make a move, she'd willingly oblige him and achieve her goal.

Stopping behind a large hedge out of the view of the other party goers, she looked up at him and moistened her lips. Fear thrummed in her veins as she waited for him to act on her signals. What if he was too honorable to help her complete her plan? For a long moment, she wondered if she would fail as the thought of marrying Thornton Sutcliffe made her heart sink.

Nikolai touched her mask, and she quickly grabbed his hand to stop him.

"No."

"How am I to give you what you've been telling me you want if I can't see your face?" he asked, his beautiful blue eyes seductively looking down at her.

"The mask must stay."

Despite his obvious confusion, her requirement didn't deter him. Gently, he pressed his lips to hers and kissed her. Annelisa's heart pounded against her chest at the thought that this was her first real kiss. Was she doing it correctly? Would he know she was experienced in this, and therefore, in what she hoped would follow and end their tryst prematurely?

As she worried about these things, Nikolai dropped his head to her neck and softly planted kisses near her collarbone. In a hoarse voice, he whispered, "Moya milaya," against her skin.

The effect of his kisses surprised her, and an unfamiliar ache began to throb inside her. She pulled his head closer to her, weaving her fingers in his thick hair, and pushed her body to his, only intensifying the ache inside.

Author's Notes

The Agony Column was a real column that appeared in the Times of London up to 1966. Located on the first page of the newspaper, it was exactly as it's been portrayed here—a collection of advertisements and notices, often cryptic, from lovers and those seeking long lost relatives, in addition to employment ads and public announcements. Often, the notices were written in foreign languages, particularly Latin, German, and French, and codes known only to the poster and respondent. During the 19th century, the column was particularly popular, most famously seen in the Arthur Conan Doyle's Sherlock Holmes Mysteries, where the world famous detective religiously combs through the ads each morning for information about cases.

The notice that appears in *Love's Master* is, in fact, from an actual advertisement that appeared in the column on Saturday, June 21, 1845. In its original form, it read, S.B. "is a STRICT Disciplinarian, and not afraid of a rather unruly Pupil." I changed it to reflect Kadar's first initial and punctuated it differently. I have no idea what the original notice referred to, but I am indebted to S.B. and his post for my initial story idea.

Qabili Palau and baklava are both dishes enjoyed in Afghanistan and deliciously easy to make. Here are recipes for both, in case you'd like to enjoy them with someone you love.

Qabili Palau

Ingredients:
- Lamb- preferably some tenderloin and shank
- Three large white onions
- Salt
- Black pepper
- Coriander powder
- Cinnamon powder
- Nutmeg powder
- Ground cumin
- Large cardamom and small cardamom powder
- Rice- basmati
- Carrots
- Raisins
- sliced almonds and pistachios
- 1/4 cup of brown sugar

Steps:

Meat:

In a large pressure cooker heat 1 cup of vegetable oil over medium high heat.

Add chopped onions and start stirring. This is one of the most important steps. Make sure that the onions do not burn, but by stirring them ever 1-2 minutes get them to a nice caramel brown color. Add meat and stir. Let cook for 2 minutes. Stir again. With each stir, add 1/4 cup of water. Repeat this stirring process until all the onion has caramelized and the meat has lost its "lamby" odor.

Now add salt ONLY. Add water to barely cover the top of the meat and pressure cook until meat is tender. Once meat is tender, over low heat, add the remainder of your spices. Turn off heat once enough water has evaporated so that you can see some of the oil on top of the meat sauce.

Carrots/raisins/nuts:

In a large frying pan place carrots. Pour 2 tablespoons of vegetable oil and the sugar on top. Cover pain and place it over a medium heat. In 2 minutes, uncover and place raisins and nuts on top of carrots without stirring and cover pot. In 1 minute, uncover and stir. Once the sugar has melted, then the mixture is ready.

Rice:

In a large pot, boil water. Add rice that has been soaked in salt- after draining it. Once rice grain is tender enough (this is a tough step to write instructions for)- then drain rice. Add drained rice back to the pot, and mix rice with the meat gravy. Use enough of the gravy so that it barely colors the rice. Do not soak the rice. Make the rice into a mound. On one side of the mound arrange the meat pieces. On the other side of the mound, bury the carrot/raisin/nuts and cover with rice.

Create ventilation holes in rice with back of utensil. Cover with large pieces of paper towel and place into a 400 Fahrenheit oven- decrease the temperature to 300 in 10 minutes- decrease the temperature to 250 in 15 minutes. Serve after 15 minutes.

Baklava

Fillo dough
1/2 pound unsalted butter
1 tsp. cinnamon
1 1/2 cups sugar
1 tsp. cardamom
Almonds
1 tsp. lemon juice
1 1/2 cups water
Crushed pistachios

First, preheat the oven to 375 degrees. Next, melt the butter over very low heat. Combine freshly ground cardamom cinnamon in a small bowl. Lay two layers of fillo dough on a baking sheet, and pour two tablespoons of melted butter over the dough. Use a pastry brush to spread the butter.

Next, sprinkle a thin layer of fresh almond nuts, and a small amount of the cinnamon/cardamom mixture. Repeat this until you have several layers. On the top layer, only spread melted butter. Bake the baklava at 375 degrees, until the fillo dough is golden brown. At this point, remove the baklava from the oven and prepare the syrup.

For the syrup... Combine one and one-half cups of water with one and one-half cups of sugar, and one teaspoon of fresh lemon juice. Bring the mix to a boil, turn down the heat and simmer for 5 minutes. While the baklava is still warm, cut it into small triangle shapes and drizzle the syrup over the baklava. To finish, sprinkle with crushed pistachio nuts.

(http://www.asiarecipe.com/afgdesserts.
html#baklava)

About the Author

K.M. Scott writes sexy contemporary romance with characters her readers love. A New York Times and USA Today bestselling author, she's been in love with romance since reading her first romance novel in junior high (she was a very curious girl!). Under her Gabrielle Bisset name, she also writes erotic historical and paranormal romance. She lives in Pennsylvania with her teenage son and a herd of animals and when she's not writing can be found reading or feeding her TV addiction.

Be sure to visit K.M.'s Facebook page at **https://www.facebook.com/kmscottauthor** for all the latest on her books, along with giveaways and other goodies! And to hear all the news on K.M. Scott books first, sign up for her newsletter today and be sure to visit her website at **http://www.kmscottbooks.com**

Visit Gabrielle's Facebook page and her website at: **http://www.gabriellebisset.com/** to find out about her books too!

Books by K.M. SCOTT:

Crash Into Me **(Heart of Stone #1)**
Fall Into Me **(Heart of Stone #2)**
Give In To Me **(Heart of Stone #3)**
The Heart of Stone Trilogy Box Set
Ever After **(A Heart of Stone Novella)**
A Heart of Stone Christmas

Temptation **(Club X #1)**
Surrender **(Club X #2)**
Possession **(Club X #3)**
Satisfaction **(Club X #4) COMING SOON!**

Silk **(Volume One)**
Silk **(Volume Two)**
Silk **(Volume Three)**
Silk **(Volume Four)**

Books by Gabrielle Bisset: